S0-BUB-973

THE FALL OF WINTER

JACK C. HALDEMAN II

science fiction

THE FALL OF WINTER

A Baen Book

Baen Enterprises
8-10 W. 36th Street
New York, N.Y. 10018

First printing, March 1985

ISBN: 0-671-55947-8

Cover art by Bob Eggleton

Printed in the United States of America

Distributed by
SIMON & SCHUSTER
MASS MERCHANDISE SALES COMPANY
1230 Avenue of the Americas
New York, N.Y. 10020

For Joe, who hears the music.

And for my friends in the deaf community, who have shown me so much about life and love. Theirs is a different music, written in the air. They are special people. Thanks.

Gainesville, Florida, 1982

CHAPTER ONE

She called it Frost. She called it home.

Teri sat transfixed as the storm rolled over the mountains and spilled into the valley of her people. She had seen hundreds of the violent squalls in her short life, yet they never ceased to fascinate her.

Above the transparent roof of the observation lounge, the sky was an angry slate gray, an uneasy calm awaiting the fury of the approaching storm. Soon the winds would come, then the rains. She wanted to go outside the dome and feel the wind, to let it rush over her body as it did the rugged land, but that was forbidden. Teri had been outside twice today and overstayed her allotment both times. Worse, Mother Lei had caught her and lectured her sternly. Though not yet an adult, Teri could no longer be considered a child. She was expected to know better.

She did know better, but that didn't change anything. She wanted to be out on Frost. Life in the closed-up dome might satisfy the Mothers, but it was bitter fruit for Teri. Life inside was no life at all. She had to feel the wind.

Teri left the observation lounge and took a lift down to the ground level. She passed several siblings as she went, muttering appropriate greetings to her brothers and sisters as they walked the halls like mirrors of each other. Slipping into a service corridor, she made her way around to the west exit. There was nothing to guard, so there were no guards. There was nothing to protect, so there were no locks. She went through the double-sealed chamber doors and stepped out into her world. The world she couldn't have.

The air was electric. The normally high ozone content of the atmosphere was charged, raising the fur on her arms and filling her with a tingle of expectation. She left their living quarters behind and walked down the path through the ever-present trees to the farm. It wasn't far.

Standing at the edge of the trees, she looked over the four square kilometers of cultivated land they called the farm. It wasn't much compared to the great mass that was Frost, but it was a start. The trees gave up ground reluctantly, fighting hard for every square meter. One moment of inattention and a sprout would break the surface. Unchecked, in a day it would be a towering plant. In a week it would be a forest, with roots so interlocked they were next to impossible to remove.

Yet this at least was a piece of land they owned. More than simply land, the farm was a promise that Frost would someday be theirs. She reached down and touched a seedling that had sprouted the previous day, one she had planted herself.

This plot of ground was seeded in bytome, a small shrub native to the sub-arctic planet Freuchen, a sister planet to Frost. The geneticists had been working with it, hoping to produce a strain that would be able to survive here. It was an excellent protein source, grew well in a harsh environment, and had a high energy conversion factor. The only trouble was that it wouldn't grow on Frost, at least not yet.

The seedling Teri touched was withered, already dying. It hadn't even survived as long as the last crop. They'd have to start over, try again. It wouldn't be the first time they'd done that, nor the last. Teri rested back on her heels as the winds picked up and watched a fluffer make its nervous way through the bytome.

Fluffers were small furry animals about half a meter tall, one of the very few native animals that had managed to survive the cataclysmic changes on Frost. They seemed to be flexible and had adapted well.

The fluffer grazed nervously as she watched, occasionally rising up on its hind legs to sniff the air. As it sniffed, its claws slid in and out of their finger sheaths, its nose folds opened and closed. She thought about chasing it from the bytome, but one fluffer couldn't do much harm. She even felt a little sympathy for it.

The small animal looked so vulnerable out in the field, its lumpy body out of place among the slender plants. It picked up a root with its multi-jointed hands and chewed it noisily, still looking around. Its large pointed ears twitched at every sound. As far as Teri knew, the fluffers had no natural enemies left on Frost, yet they always seemed to be on edge.

Suddenly the fluffer scampered off toward the trees. They always headed for the trees when they were frightened. Even though they had no tails they were excellent climbers and ran through the branches just as easily as they ran on the ground. A cold gust of wind hit Teri and made her eyes water. She stood and faced the distant mountains.

The temperature was dropping rapidly as overhead the sky churned. Distant thunder rolled and crashed across the valley, shaking Teri where she stood. To the west the clouds split cleanly into several groups, as if a giant finger had come down from the heavens and traced lines across the sky. She knew it was the work of the satellites, but that didn't make it any less wondrous.

Teri ruffled her fur against the cold and coughed a deep, rasping cough. She pulled at the collar of her simple one-piece suit, closing it tightly. Her eyes stung and filled with water. She had stayed out too long today, too many times, and would pay for it. Pay for it in physical pain and discomfort as well as having to endure the ranting and raving of the Mothers. It was a toss-up as to which was worse. Still, she could stand them both, as she had so many times in the past.

Mother Lei called her wild and irresponsible. Teri knew it was only that she had a dream, a dream she would not let go of.

Teri looked for the fluffer and hoped it was safe in the trees. They were such skittish animals, afraid of everything. Maybe that was how they had survived. She closed her eyes and felt the wind. The air had a sharp taste to it, metallic. For a moment, with her eyes tightly closed, she almost seemed to be a part of the planet. Then she gagged on the metallic taste in her mouth and the rains started, a cold acid rain that stung as it hit and stained her pelt. Mother Lei would be furious.

Hatred and frustration welled up inside her, spilled over. Hatred toward the planet she loved, frustration at having her time there parceled out in minutes. Her ear flaps closed reflexively and she looked to the sky, raising her fists toward the clouds in anger.

This was her planet. She was born to live here and no place else. This was her home, and she couldn't have it.

"It's not fair," she cried out in desperation, choking back her sobs. As the caustic rain washed over Teri, the fluffer watched her from the protection of the trees.

Its gaze never wavered, its eyes never blinked.

For ages upon eons Frost had lain untouched; a cold, hard lump of frozen rock stuck in a distant, unimportant star system, too far from its parent sun to have developed more than rudimentary life. It hung in space undisturbed, foreboding, patiently circling the star that gave it only feeble warmth. It waited for man, and man came.

It was the wrong planet in the right place. It was far too cold and what atmosphere it had was deadly poisonous. The planet was inhospitable, but the location was ideal. It orbited near one of the rare phase-shift points that were scattered throughout the universe. These physical anomalies made interstellar travel possible. Wormholes. Mankind needed the planet and what it needs it finds a way to take, usually with force.

And force was what it took, in huge quantities. The cold tranquility of the planet was shattered after millions of years of silence. A comet was snatched from its lazy orbit at the fringes of the star system and directed to impact on Frost, forever changing the basic nature of the planet. The energy involved was enormous, the results massive in scale.

The planet shifted in its orbit, tilted on its axis, changed its speed of rotation. Mountain ranges rose and fell, land masses rearranged themselves. The comet brought more water to the planet. It brought badly needed trace elements. It brought calculated destruction.

Large asteroids were maneuvered to the planet, crashed to its surface. Others were kept in orbit to supply raw materials for the operation. Long-dormant volcanos erupted, and the land was scoured and torn apart. Massive amounts of dust and ash filled the air, causing the temperature of the planet to fluctuate. Frost shook and trembled in the grip of immense forces as it struggled to reach an equilibrium.

The asteroids brought into orbit around the planet were mined. Manufacturing bases and living quarters were built on the larger ones; the smaller ones were broken into pieces. From these hunks of rock and ice the raw materials for the project on Frost were extracted.

A string of huge solar mirrors was constructed, stretching out like a sparkling necklace in space. A hundred kilometers on a side, the mirrors collected the star's feeble light, concentrated it, and beamed it down to selected sites on the planet's surface. Frost grew warmer. It developed an equatorial ocean that was ice-free a good part of the year.

Only then did machinery and men descend on Frost. They worked the land over, built a few small structures. Relentlessly they attacked the planet's surface, attempting to make Frost what it wasn't: habitable.

But the men who worked there could never live on Frost or walk on the planet unaided. That was for others.

It would take a thousand years to make Frost into an Earth-like planet. They didn't have the time—they wanted it now. They had allotted 150 years for the project. If they hadn't finished by then they would regroup and cut their losses. Frost would be chalked up as a bad investment and they'd salvage what they could. But they wanted it badly. They were giving it all they had.

When they finished they would still have a planet that was too cold for comfortable human life. The atmosphere would still be poisonous. That didn't particularly worry them. They were working on that, too.

But Frost had other plans. It didn't give up easily.

He hadn't heard of Frost. Not yet.

Roger Trent touched the sore spot on his throat where Doc Grinnell had removed the filters this morning. He could have rested today, probably should have, but Sam had wanted to bust loose a little. After three stinking months on New Hope it sounded like a fine idea, one of Sam's best.

Sam was Roger's pilot. Madge Grinnell was his doctor. Roger Trent was a specialist in his own way, a man often in demand. Right now all he wanted was another beer to wash the dirt and grime of New Hope from his throat. He gestured to the bartender across the room. The man nodded, started to pull the beer from an old-fashioned tap.

The bar Sam had selected was dimly lit and crowded, with maybe fifty or sixty conversations going on at once. It seemed loud to Roger, but he knew that it wasn't. It was all an illusion. Not a single word was being spoken aloud for the simple reason that there was practically no one in the pub capable of hearing speech. This was a pilot's bar. Pilots were deaf.

Roger laughed at a joke Drifter Pete was telling, his face contorted with mock surprise at the punch line. Drifter Pete could tell a story like no one else. He used his light-studded hands, his face, his entire body to tell a story, embellish it, act it out. He gave his tales so much depth and spirit that they would have paled considerably if translated into mere words. The rambling account he had just finished was a highly improbable—and physically impossible—conjecture on the mating habits of the colonists on Random. Drifter Pete had been around and he liked his stories raunchy.

The bartender brought over Roger's beer. Sam was right on his heels. The pilot pulled out a chair and draped his lanky body into it, hands flashing as he joined the several conversations going on simultaneously around the table. He was already a little glassy-eyed, and with good reason. He'd had to stay in orbit alone most of the three months Roger was on New Hope. It was hard not to get a little batty under those conditions, and he was trying to get it out of his system. It felt good to be around people again.

Roger watched Sam and grinned. They'd been together a long time and knew each other well. Sam was an excellent pilot, but all pilots were excellent. Sam was more than that. Sam was a friend.

Pilots were, out of necessity, totally deaf. They were either born that way or made that way, usually the latter. A hearing person simply could not maneuver a ship through the phase points and come out whole. It had been tried, of course, but the pilots had all returned barely alive with no minds left at all. Though there were technical names for what happened to them, most people called them victims of the Siren's Song. Either way, they were as good as dead.

Machines were no better. They couldn't handle it alone. Human guidance was necessary, critical. No automatically piloted ship had ever made it safely through the wormholes from one phase-shift point to another. It took a special kind of human to detect the subtle interactions of the power fields, to feel the delicate balances between constantly changing forces, to guide the ship through the confusion of warped space to its destination.

Pilots had to be part artist, part technician, part craftsman. They had to be coolly logical, yet sensitive enough to detect minute shifts in their equipment. They were special people, relatively few in number, and incredibly important.

Right this moment, Sam didn't look all that important. Mostly he looked a little sloshed. Roger took it in good humor and ordered a round for the table. Sam slid lower in his chair, a sheepish grin spreading across his deceptively boyish face.

Sam looked twenty and probably wouldn't change much for a long time. He had one of those faces that never seems to age. Actually, he was only a couple of years younger than Roger. At times he envied people like Drifter Pete, whose lives had etched deep lines across their faces. At other times he used his youthful appearance to great advantage, especially when he was out carousing. Women seemed to like it, and he certainly couldn't complain about that.

In spite of his young looks, Sam had the unmistakable appearance of a pilot. His entire body, especially his head, was covered with tattooed dots that marked the attachment points for the wiring harness he wore while in control of the ship. Like most pilots, he wore his hair long in direct opposition to current tastes. Even with careful combing he wasn't able to hide the treated patches on his scalp where no hair would ever grow. The electrodes needed good contact points.

The most striking thing about Sam was his hands. They glowed. Surgically implanted light crystals outlined his hands and fingers. It wasn't cosmetic, though stranger things were being done in the name of fashion, especially on the newer planets. He talked with his hands and the crystal studs allowed him to talk in the dark. His were pale yellow.

Chris was talking about the group of colonists she had just ferried to Babylon. Hard-shelled religious types, they had refused to go under for phase-shift transfer. She had tried to tell them it was just like sleeping. That was the usual line you fed first-timers—a lie of course, it was more like death—but it hadn't worked. She ended up faking an ejection drill and gassed them in their pods. Instead of reviving them immediately after the transfer, she kept them down until they were almost to the planet. It proved to be a wise decision, since they were mad as hell when they came out of it. They ranted and raved, beat their breasts, talked briefly of mass suicide. They felt they'd been soiled, ruined. Chris had hoped the sight of Babylon large in the viewscreens would get them excited and take their minds off how they had been tricked. It worked, after a fashion. She was convinced that if she had wakened them at the exit point, with Babylon still a good two weeks away, they would have killed each other long before they reached the planet. Or worse, killed her.

They laughed at the silly superstitions of the colonists, yet they knew that pilots were far more superstitious than any other group of people. They each had their own private collection of rituals and habits. Sam wore a small medallion on a leather thong around his neck. Chris wore an ivory ring on her little finger. Drifter Pete always donned the same jump suit for each transfer. They preferred to call these actions idiosyncrasies, but by any other name they would be superstitions. Still, you couldn't blame them for their quirks. If anything went wrong in a phase-shift transfer, it went all-the-way wrong. Mistakes were invariably fatal.

All this was far from their minds as they relaxed in the Earthside bar. Time between jumps went quickly. They worked hard and, when they had time, played hard.

The round Roger had ordered arrived, followed quickly by another bought by Drifter Pete. It was getting late. The lights grew even dimmer. Chris's hands were faint blue blurs as she talked. The glasses piled up on the table. It was going to be a long night.

She lived on Frost but was not a part of it. It could never be her home.

Mother Lei looked at Teri and shook her head in bitter frustration. Would the child never learn? It had to be this child, time after time, not one of the others.

"I'm sorry," said the young girl. "I didn't realize the rains would come so fast."

"That's no excuse. You had no business being out there in the first place." Mother Lei was nearly half a meter taller than Teri and her features were much sharper.

"It won't happen again," said Teri, looking up from the couch.

"You said that last time and the time before that. It carries no weight with me. You could have been killed. If you were supposed to be out more often you would be scheduled for it. The topsiders would see to that."

"Scheduled! What do they know about *any-thing*?"

"Easy, child. They know everything about Frost and everything about you."

"They may have their heads full of chemical equations, but they don't know fluff-drops about people. About us."

"Teri! I won't allow such talk. We owe them a lot."

"We owe them nothing."

Mother Lei gritted her teeth. How sharp this child's tongue was. Disrespect was typical of her generation, but Teri carried it to extreme lengths. She paused to give Teri a chance to calm down, and when she spoke, it was in a softer voice.

"You know I have to punish you. What do you think would be suitable?"

Teri squirmed on the couch, looking uncomfortable. She avoided Mother Lei's eyes and said nothing.

"I think you might learn something with two weeks confinement," she said to the girl.

Teri looked up sharply. "No. Anything else," she cried. "I can't stand to be cooped up in here."

"I realize that. Perhaps that will drive the lesson home. You will be allowed to leave only during the regularly scheduled acclimation periods. You are to be escorted at all times during these periods. You will not be allowed outside alone, nor at any time above the minimum the topsiders require."

Teri was trying to hold her anger back, but

not succeeding very well. It would serve no purpose to lose her temper. It would only make things worse.

"Is that all?" she asked, biting off the words.

"Yes."

"May I leave now?"

"Yes."

The young girl stood, quivering with suppressed anger and frustration. Her pelt was bleached in spots from the acid rain. She left the room.

Mother Lei sat down with a sigh. She realized that she had probably been too harsh with Teri, as usual. It was hard for her not to be. The girl was a trial. The fact that she was Teri's womb-mother only served to complicate the situation. She knew the rules. Womb-mothers weren't supposed to get involved.

Teri had started as an egg implanted in her womb. That was the beginning and end of it. The egg may have started as one of her own, but by the time it was reimplanted, already fertilized, it had been considerably modified. The topsiders had done it—the ones who came and went in cumbersome suits, the ones who told them what to do and when to do it, the ones who controlled their lives. The ones who had created their lives.

Their goal was a race of people who could live unaided on Frost, that much she knew. She, and all those who had gone before her, were simply a means of producing the generation that could survive outside—Teri's generation. They would go on and live, explore, and tame the planet. They would multiply. Mother Lei and her sisters would die inside and be forgotten.

There were no males before Teri's generation, for none were needed. Lei's ova had been removed, analyzed, manipulated, and fertilized with a specific cross-match of genes to produce exactly what the topsiders wanted: a generation like Teri.

The end result was that Teri was of Lei, but was not exactly like her. Externally the differences were obvious, but not startling. Teri was at least half a meter shorter than the Mothers. She was stockier, heavier. Her bones were denser, her muscles larger. Both her ear and eye flaps closed completely and her pelt was considerably thicker.

Internally her metabolism was subtly different from that of Mother Lei. Many of the poisons in Frost's atmosphere were not harmful to her at all. Some were, in fact, necessary for Teri to live. She had to spend at least an hour a day outside to pick them up. They called these excursions acclimation periods. Teri loved them and wished they were longer and more frequent. In this case, unfortunately, too much of a good thing would prove fatal.

Frost was still in a state of flux. Its atmosphere wasn't coming into line like it should have. At the same time Teri couldn't live her entire life inside the dome. In a different way—but just as surely—it was slowly poisoning her system. She was caught in the middle.

Mother Lei felt that her own generation was

the one caught in the middle. They had simply been vessels to bring this last generation into existence and now they were being ignored, discarded.

They had always, it seemed, been ignored. Their education had been haphazard and spotty, generally provided by the Mothers of the generation before them. The children, on the other hand, were educated primarily by the topsiders. It was no wonder they had such strange ideas.

Mother Lei buried her face in her hands and sighed. She had a splitting headache. Tension. She wished she hadn't been so hard on Teri. She wished she could express the emotions she felt instead of holding them inside.

Her Mothers had all died at about forty years of age. They were such a short-lived people. Why did the years have to be filled with so much pain?

He called it work. To him it was just a job.

The great globe that was Frost hung above his head as he drifted easily from a tether attached to the substructure of a microwave transmission satellite. The view failed to impress him. He was bored.

The five-year hitch hadn't seemed like it would be too much when he had signed on at Paragon. The pay was good and there sure as hell wasn't anyplace to spend it out here. He'd be flush when his tour ended, if he lasted that long. It was a boring job and he had one standard year left to go.

It was always the same, day after day, year after year. Hurry up, then wait. Except for the pay he might as well be in the Service. At least that way he'd get leave once in a while.

He didn't give a healthy drop for the planet or the people he worked for. As long as the pay came regularly he'd keep plugging away, no more, no less. As for the freaks down there, he was just as glad he didn't have anything to do with them. Damn bioforms were just like slugs—or worse. Chimeras. They weren't even human anymore. Let 'em muck around in their own slime. That wasn't any of his business.

He just kept the machines working. He'd probably die with a spanner in his hand at some crummy job just like this.

Even the food was rotten.

Doctor Madge Grinnell found them in the back room collapsed over a card table covered with chits and markers. An empty bottle of rotgut tequila sat in the middle of the table like a wino's centerpiece. Madge wasn't surprised. It had happened before.

For the last three hours she'd been trying to rouse Roger on his implanted alarm. He'd have to be dead or passed out to ignore the throbbing tooth. Knowing how he and Sam sometimes behaved after a job, she'd have put money on the latter.

It hadn't been hard to track them down. They had their regular haunts. This was a pretty high-class place compared to some of the others. They probably hadn't even been mugged. Too bad, it might have taught them a lesson.

Madge selected a cartridge from the little black pouch on her belt and sprayed the underside of Sam's left arm. She waited until the medication took effect and he clawed his way up from the depths of his stupor. Out of spite, she left Roger in his miserable state. After all, she'd spent the last three hours chasing him down.

"I feel awful," signed Sam, moving his hands with painful slowness. He looked it.

"You should," signed Madge. "You two try to drink this place dry?"

Sam attempted to flash his impish grin, but a sharp pain ripped through his forehead. "We gave it our best shot," he signed.

"I'll bet. Give me a hand with the basket case, will you?"

Sam helped her pull Roger to his feet. He was woozy and uncooperative.

"Don't you have anything for my head?" Sam asked. "I'm in terrible shape."

"My heart bleeds for you," signed Madge. "You'll just have to suffer until we get home. Let's move." Sam was in no condition to object.

It took them ten minutes to get to the nearest tube station. Roger wasn't exactly helping. From there it was another forty minutes to their home in the Keys. Two thousand kilometers. It seemed a lot longer to Roger as he slowly came around—more like light years.

Madge deposited her charges in their quarters and gave them what medication they required. She left them to fix their own black coffee—the ultimate cure—and retired to her wing of the sprawling house, leaving word for Roger to call. An hour later he buzzed her and they met on the veranda outside his suite, overlooking the ocean.

"Sorry," said Roger, sipping his fourth cup of coffee.

"You bucking for a new liver?" she asked.

"Nothing like that. Just letting off a little steam. You know how it is."

"I'm afraid I do. You've got to cut that stuff out." She was needling him, still feeling a little spiteful for having to track him down. It was a rare occurrence. Usually Roger was as reliable and as stable as a rock. But whenever it happened, it happened big and it was always with Sam.

"You could have come along. We invited you."

"No thanks. Self-destruction isn't one of my strong points. I don't take transplants like you do."

"Are you making fun of my metabolism again?" asked Roger.

Madge laughed. "No, silly. It's just that this is the only liver I'll ever have and I've got to take care of it."

"Through with the lecture?"

"Guess so. They never do much good, anyway." Below the veranda the ocean rolled with a soft murmur against the beach. The moon was full, the water silver in the dim light.

When industry had moved into space, Earth had become a lot quieter and cleaner. Roger liked that. It was one of the main reasons he made it his home, at least for the short times he was able to spend there. A satellite traced a lazy line across the clear sky. Roger set his coffee cup on the railing.

"So what's up? Why the Dick Tracy act?"

"Ever hear of Frost?"

"What kind of frost?"

"A planet. That kind of Frost."

Roger shook his head. "Never heard of it. What's that got to do with us?"

"Terraforming operation. Work."

Roger moaned. "Come on, you've got to be kidding. We just got back." He'd been looking forward to at least a couple of months of taking it easy.

Madge ignored him. "It's a big operation," she said. "Headed by that group on Paragon. Unity Alliance—you remember them. They picked up the option on your contract. You really don't have any choice."

Roger had done some minor climatology work for them on a small planet they were mining. He hadn't liked it very much. The people who hired him had been cold and calculating. Just like them to pick up his option, damn it.

"The pay?"

"Astronomical, with a generous time bonus. They seem to be in a hurry."

"Isn't everyone?"

Madge shook her head. "Atmospheric imbalance, among other things. Looks complicated. They've got a bunch of bioforms on site. Chimeras."

Roger looked up sharply. Planning to inhabit. That meant automatic control, absolute control. It *was* a big operation. "They send the data?" he asked.

"Dumped it a couple of hours ago. I filed it away. The access code is FROST:SAVE."

"Tacky, Madge," he said with a grin.

"You don't pay me enough to be a secretary," she said good-naturedly. "I have my hands full just playing doctor, patching you up all the time."

"When do we leave?"

"They've got pull, I have to hand them that. They managed to cut a lot of red tape. We're scheduled as a priority-two for phase insertion."

"So when do we leave?" Damn it, he hadn't even had time to get his Earth legs back.

"We're booked for the 0800 shuttle."

He looked miserable. "Tomorrow?"

She tapped her watch, shook her head. "Today," she said. "Seven hours."

Roger sighed, reached for his coffee. It was cold. A group of night birds squawked as they skimmed over the ocean's dark surface. He stood up and stretched, looked out over the water. He never got to spend enough time here. "We'd better get started," he said.

They turned their backs on the moon-

splashed ocean and went inside the house.
There was a lot of work to be done.

Teri was watching the 'rooms. She had managed to slip away from Lan, who was supposed to be keeping an eye on her. It wasn't
hard. He was easily distracted outside, as they
all were. After all, it was their home, or at
least the promise of their home. They wanted
as much of it as possible, for as long a time as
they could manage.

The mushrooms towered over her, fifteen
meters high, their ridged stalks easily two
meters in diameter. They were topped by huge
caps, fluted on the underside, smooth and
sticky on top. Teri was fascinated by the
'rooms, but she gave them a wide berth. They
were living terraforming tools. They were also
omnivorous.

By day the 'rooms were fully extended, at-
tracting and trapping flying creatures with
their sticky skin. At night the stalks contracted
and the button tops settled to the ground. The
caps covered a circle more than six meters in
diameter and dissolved any plant or animal
life underneath. The 'rooms also had a limited mobility, each able to cover a range of
about forty square meters over its lifetime.
When one died, it composted itself into nutrients favorable to the terraforming effort. The
farm had been cleared, for the most part, by
use of the 'rooms. They could handle small
trees, but not the full-grown ones, of course.

Where Teri stood she could see about twenty

of them, carefully spaced out over a small field. In the twilight, their stalks were just beginning to contract, casting long twisted shadows across the ground. It gave her an uneasy feeling. They were odd plants, not of Earth, not of Frost, but the products of the geneticists, much as she was.

Yet Teri felt no kinship with them, only a vague fear, mixed with awe. The buttons were covered with small trapped insects, mostly lacewings. Some were still flapping, some partially digested.

Even though she feared them, the 'rooms were her allies in the fight to conquer Frost. There were others: the plankton rafts that she'd seen from the beach once or twice, and the deep-fish and the webs that she'd only heard about. They were all part of the complicated, multipronged attack on the planet.

She turned down the path to rejoin the group. Lan would not report her missing as long as she got back before their time was up. He'd get in as much trouble as she would.

Actually, Lan probably wouldn't report her absence no matter how long she was gone. A natural bond had developed over the years between all her brothers and sisters. They tended to protect each other whenever possible against the intrusion of the Mothers and topsiders. Sharing both blood and desire, they stuck together. It was that simple.

Yet lately Teri had noticed a subtle shift in the way her siblings felt about her. Most of her brothers and sisters seemed to defer to her when decisions were made. They asked her opinion on just about everything, as if it were better than theirs. At times it embarrassed her, as though they were somehow seeking her approval. She didn't know quite what to make of it. It looked as if they were seeking a leader and thrusting her into that role without even asking her about it. It made her uncomfortable, and a little angry sometimes. She didn't like leaders, any leaders. It was enough that they all shared a desire for the planet. There shouldn't be a need for any more than that.

In the dim light of the sloping path, an exposed root caught her foot and tripped her. She fell to the ground, unhurt.

Standing, Teri kicked at the root. It was a futile gesture—the root wouldn't budge. Each root had a hundred other roots coming off it, burying themselves deep into the ground. The plant, like all things on Frost, held deeply to life, to survival.

She heard the voices of the others and walked toward them, thinking of the root and her own desires to live on the planet she knew as home. Only time would tell who would come out on top. The only sure thing was that it would be a bitter fight, all the way to the end.

CHAPTER TWO

Roger felt as though he had wheels permanently strapped to the seat of his pants. It seemed he was always on the go.

He didn't relax until after they'd left the near-Earth way station and docked with the transport that would take them to the phase-shift point and their waiting ship, located just beyond the orbit of Pluto. It would take them a week and a half to get there.

The transport was one of the large ones, built to hold a hundred people, a thousand if they were sleepers, stacked on top of each other like cords of firewood. The three of them were the only people on board except for the crew, and they rattled around inside the huge ship like seeds in a gourd, not used to the luxury of having whole suites of rooms available on this leg of a trip. Usually they had to share a single cubicle, sleeping in shifts on the single narrow bed. The group on Paragon had chartered the transport, it being the only ship available on such short notice.

If Unity Alliance wanted to throw their money around, Roger wasn't going to complain. He set up a work area in the day room, taking over a terminal there. He'd been running through the dump on Frost. It was a complicated operation, like most of them were.

Terraforming was usually carried out on near Earth-normal planets. Discovery of the phase-shift points had opened up a multitude of other planets to man. In most cases it was only a matter of adjusting a few factors to make the planet habitable. They weren't always comfortable, but they were livable, providing opportunities for man to expand.

Occasionally, for various reasons, it was necessary or desirable to terraform a difficult planet, one far from Earth-normal. That was the case with Frost.

Frost's orbit passed very close to a phase-shift point. In terms of shipping costs and energy requirements alone this made the planet extremely desirable. Phase-shift points were nearly always a considerable distance from any planet. There were other factors at work, too. Some of them gave Roger an uneasy feeling.

The fact that Unity had developed chimeras for the planet could complicate things. He questioned their motives in taking such an obviously expensive gamble. It would have been much easier to simply establish a series of bases there. They must have a lot riding on the planet to want such complete control.

Most of the factors were purely practical matters. The planet had atmospheric problems. They'd no sooner get one system in line than another would swing out of balance. The nitrogen cycle was a mess. He could see they had big problems. Of course, if they hadn't, they never would have called him in. He didn't come cheap.

Roger was a troubleshooter, a specialist who dealt in large-scale operations. The more complex they were, the better he liked them. It was like solving detective puzzles with only a few fuzzy clues. He enjoyed his work, but he'd never intended to get into it in the first place. It was something that just sort of happened to him.

Part of it had to do with his photographic memory, and part with the fact that he was easily bored. He'd spent most of his time in school staring out the window, never managing to stay with any one subject for long. The fact that he never forgot anything he read or heard got him through, and his curiosity kept him going. As it turned out, he knew a lot of things about a lot of subjects rather than having any one speciality. He had an eclectic mind and he used it.

Terraforming operations were extremely complex, a strange mixture of arts and sciences, a blend of tremendous forces, delicate balances, and subtle shifts. They brought together biologists, physicists, geneticists, geologists, architects, astronomers, environmental engineers, politicians, ecologists—the list was nearly endless.

For a successful operation, everyone had to work in harmony, because a miscalculation anywhere along the line would disrupt the entire operation. Everything was so interrelated that it was often difficult to pinpoint the original mistake, and the majority of the people working on the project knew little or nothing beyond their specialties. That was where people like Roger fit in. He was hired to find out what went wrong, and—if possible—tell them how to fix it. There weren't many people like him. Roger knew of four others, one of whom was making threatening noises about getting out of the business and finding himself a quiet place on a quiet planet. Roger couldn't blame him. It was a hectic life.

But Roger was unusually well-suited for such a life, and he owed it all to his parents, parents he'd never seen. Roger was the offspring of one of the early lines of chimeras—bioformed people genetically altered to live on other worlds. He was supposed to be special, but he turned out to be more than that. He was unique.

Something had happened deep in the twisted maze of the genes that produced Roger. The geneticists never found out what it was, and they were never able to duplicate it.

Roger's body was exceptionally resilient and adaptable. He had a near-zero tissue rejection cofactor, and he was a rapid healer. His body had never rejected a transplant, no matter how foreign. He was a universal donor and could accept blood from any source. His defense mechanisms never reacted against surgical implants, and he had several.

He was a bioengineer's dream come true.

With proper modification he could breathe poisons, endure extremely harsh conditions. Using an exoframe, he could walk in crushing gravities. His metabolism could be speeded up or slowed nearly to a stop.

On top of all this he was intelligent. He could see answers where others could see only questions.

These things were drawing him toward Frost. Frost was waiting.

Among those waiting on Frost was Jud Walsh, and he was worried. It was his responsibility to see that the operation on Frost was successfully completed on schedule. It looked like he wasn't going to make it, and he was feeling the pressure.

Walsh wasn't a scientist and he had never had any desire to be one. He was an administrator, one of the best. He left the details to people who were good at details. It was his job to oversee the project and make sure all the pieces fit, and they weren't fitting well at all.

He stood up from his desk terminal and paced the small office. An individual room was a luxury out in the field, one of the perks of the position he held. Long ago, when he had been a young man, it had seemed like quite a status symbol to him, like the key to the executive washroom. Now it was just a part of his life. It didn't even begin to make up for the static he was getting or the grief that came crashing down on his head day after day.

Most of the pressure was coming from Paragon. The board of directors was getting twitchy, and that was no surprise. The consortium had a lot of time and money invested here. It would take two hundred years for Frost to show a profit, even if everything worked out as planned. If it didn't, there'd be hell to pay. Walsh knew he'd be on the receiving end of any drop that came down the tube.

The governments of five planets formed the Unity Alliance consortium that was in charge of the terraforming operation on Frost. They were the people that Walsh answered to.

Two of the planets were in the Paragon system, two more were out by Hell's Gate. The other was a planet called Transit. They were connected by phase-shift points and economic ties. Frost was a plum, a jewel. No planet this close to a phase-shift point had ever been discovered before. It would be worth a lot to control it.

But that wasn't enough. If control was all they wanted, they could have legally done that by establishing a ground base and a satellite system. But that would have meant that others could use the planet, too. That they most emphatically didn't want. Therefore, the chimeras. It was all nice and legal. Self-sufficient lifeforms on any planet had total authority over the planet.

The chimeras would own Frost and Unity Alliance would own them, at least for the next twenty generations. It was an airtight contract, simple and legal.

But first the chimeras had to be able to live there. The way things were going, it didn't look like they would.

A soft chime rang on his desk and a male voice interrupted his nervous pacing.

"Incoming fax from Paragon, Mr. Walsh. Do you want hard copy or should I file it?"

Jud Walsh walked to his desk and waved the intercom open. "Both," he said. "I'll file the flimsy."

"Very good, Mr. Walsh."

As he scanned the display, the flimsy slid noiselessly from its slot. More bad news from Paragon. At least that troubleshooter was on his way. He was supposed to be the best.

Walsh fervently hoped so.

Madge was hooking Sam into the guidance system. He winced as she slid the arterial needle into the tap for his atrial catheter. It hurt. That was one of the few connections that couldn't be preplaced. It had to be inserted separately every time. A direct pathway to the heart was simply too dangerous to leave in place.

They were on their own ship now, having left the transport ten hours ago. It had taken them that long to get everything organized.

On such short notice they hadn't been able to set things up in advance.

Madge was glad that Roger was already under. For the last three days he'd been unbearable, fidgeting over everything, picking at unimportant details, as if nobody was qualified to do anything but him. He was impatient, that was all. He nearly always was. Once he'd digested all the information they had on Frost, he couldn't wait to get started.

Much as he groused about Unity picking up his option, once he'd started looking into their problem he'd gotten interested, excited. The little boy in him was most impatient. He couldn't wait to get his hands on Frost. Madge smiled at the thought. That was the one thing she really liked about Roger. Once he settled into something, he devoted all his energy to it. He was a competent, dedicated worker and Madge liked working along with him.

Roger's ship, the *Kodiak Bear*, didn't look like a ship at all, at least not in the conventional sense. It lacked the streamlined aerodynamics characteristic of ships that had to take off or land in planetary atmospheres. Nor did it have the stark, functional style of the transports and barges that never felt the strong tug of gravity. It looked like two huge doughnuts set at right angles to each other with a tinker toy mobile suspended in the middle. It wasn't designed to be pretty, just to get the job done.

The doughnuts were modified plasma accelerators, their fields carefully adjusted. The mobile held the crew and the controls. The phase-shift point provided the initial energy, and Sam did the fine-tuning through the wormhole to the other side.

Three other ships hung seemingly motionless around the invisible phase-shift point. They were all considerably larger than the *Kodiak Bear*.

"Where's all that TLC you bedside jocks are supposed to be famous for?" signed Sam as Madge tried to untangle the leads on the primary cranial harness. "I thought you were supposed to be gentle, loving folk."

"Stop moving around like that," mouthed Madge, her hands full. She spoke slowly and faced him. Sam had been a hearing person most of his life. His auditory nerves had been removed near the end of his training. He could read lips very well. "If you don't sit still I might decide you need a number eight Maxwell."

A Maxwell was a urine catheter. Number eight was huge, the largest size they came in. Sam winced in mock horror, but he quit moving, too.

Madge had been with Roger a long time, longer even than Sam. She had initially been attracted to him by curiosity—any doctor would give her eyeteeth for a chance to mess around with someone as biologically complex as Roger. She had stayed for other reasons, reasons every bit as complex as Roger's unique metabolism.

Preparing Sam for flight was only one of her jobs, a minor one at that. She also had to ready herself and Roger, along with any passengers they might be carrying. But that was trivial work, simple basic life-support systems. Anyone could be trained to do that.

Basically Madge was a surgeon, though her undergraduate studies had been heavy on bioengineering. She used both when it came to her real job: Roger.

On New Hope, their last trip out, Roger's modifications had been fairly simple, but delicate. The high levels of caustic ash in the atmosphere had required that she implant tracheal filters in addition to the nasal ones. They'd had to be replaced several times. Overlays had been inserted to protect his eyes. Polarized for the glare on New Hope, they also cut out radiation at potentially harmful wavelengths. He'd had to wear a Schaffer Bag, a device that fit on the small of his back and tapped into his superior vena cava. It acted like a pair of super kidneys, drawing out poisons unique to New Hope from his system. She'd adjusted his pacemaker for a resting heartrate of 120 beats per minute. He'd burned up one hell of a lot of energy on New Hope. Too bad he hadn't had enough time for a decent rest on Earth. All in all, from her end, New Hope hadn't been too difficult. Not nearly as bad as that time on Faith. She could only guess at what Frost would be like. They were all different.

Her relationship with Roger was complicated; doctor/patient on one hand, employee/boss on the other, and all the shades in

between. They were professionally equal, both
very good in their chosen fields. Madge tended
to baby Roger a little at times. He was fairly
disorganized and, being a precise person, she
couldn't stand that. Over the years she'd drifted
into the position of taking care of the odds
and ends of their operation simply because
Roger made such a mess of them. If she'd left
everything to him, it would have fallen apart a
long time ago. She didn't really mind.

What it boiled down to was that they had
become friends over the years, close friends.
They'd been just about everything but lovers.
Somehow that had never seemed . . . well . . .
appropriate.

She fussed with the leads that ran to Sam's
skull. They were small stick-on electrodes.
Fragile-looking wafers, each had a thin color-
coded wire that ran into the back of Sam's
chair. Some would gather data from the sensors and feed it to Sam, others would gather
information from Sam and feed it back to the
ship. In a very real way Sam, while piloting
the ship, would become part of the ship
himself.

Some of the wires picked up impulses from
the scalp surface, some of them—led by thin
platinum wires imbedded deep in Sam's
brain—picked up or delivered information to
other, more deeply buried areas.

The phase-shift points had, at first, seemed
to be a contradiction to normal physical laws,
but upon examination turned out to be a con-
firmation of them. Time and space were like

Siamese twins—normal when they were apart, intermingled and warped when they were forced into close proximity. Some people called the connections through the phase-shift points wormholes, and that's what they were—wormholes to another place in the physical universe, a subway through twisted space that warped time around itself.

An objective observer would have seen one of the phase-shift transfers as instantaneous, but to the people inside they were far from that. Depending on the route, the pilot would experience a subjective time of anywhere from forty-eight hours on upward. The longest one to date had lasted two weeks. The pilot was a babbling idiot when they pulled him from the ship. Not even the most highly trained person imaginable could have stood so much strain for so long.

The pilot had absolutely no chance to relax during the time within the wormhole. The chair he sat in was an integral part of the guidance system of the ship. His arms rested in slings, his fingers slipped into individual sheaths. Specific combinations of finger movements controlled the direction of the ship as it made its delicate way through the shifting forces. Movements of his eyes guided a small reflective laser to sensitive areas on the goggles he wore, imparting still more information to the ship. The ship in turn conveyed information to him not only by dials and gauges, but by pressure applied to certain parts of his body, his back, his arms. It was more than a human could bear, so the human became less human, more machine. At the same time the machine that was the ship became more human. It was a trade-off.

Sam's physical condition would be carefully monitored and adjusted by the ship. Chemicals would keep him awake, alert. Machines would drain the waste products and accumulated poisons from his constantly fatiguing body. Everything but his mind would be kept stable and at rest.

That was the strain that Sam and all pilots had to face each time they took a ship through the wormholes. Some of them didn't make it that far. Nine out of ten prospective pilots were weeded out in the first few months. Over half of the remainder went through the years of intensive training only to discover they couldn't handle the constant tension. There was no stigma attached to failing. It was a long road, and hard. Only the best made it.

Madge finished attaching the harness. Sam was nearly immobilized by a maze of wires and sensors. She looked around in front of him and touched his nose for luck. It was a ritual so old neither of them could remember when she had started it.

"Good luck," she said quietly. Reading her lips, Sam smiled back at her. His mouth was about the only part of him that could move freely.

Madge backed away, looking at her friend strapped in his chair. Like all other non-pilots, she wondered what it felt like to be awake during transit. Sometimes she fantasized about it, dreamed about it.

In her dreams it was like riding a powerful white stallion through a multicolored rain. She dove through clouds and soared far from land. Sometimes the horse became the ship, sometimes it was both. She reached for stars as if they were brass rings and she was a girl again on a carousel in some dream-house carnival where the lights were always soft and the music never ended. She was embarrassed by these dreams and never told anyone about them. They happened more often than she liked to admit, even to herself.

But the dreams vanished upon awakening and reality took over. There was no way she could tell what it was *really* like. Some of the non-pilots thought it must be a terrible experience, others thought it had to be beautiful. Whatever it felt like it was an experience that could only be shared by pilots. That didn't keep her from wondering, though, and feeling more than a little jealous.

As she left Sam, she checked Roger in his capsule. He was sleeping; all his signs looked good. She climbed into her own capsule, next to his, and lowered the lid.

With a practiced movement that was the result of years of experience, she found the twin leads in the darkness. One was a thick tube, the other a small wire. She attached the thick one to the tap embedded in the back of her neck, the thin one to a small shaved place behind her left ear.

As a matter of convenience she had installed permanent taps on all three of them. Most regular users of the wormholes had them; it was a lot easier than jabbing yourself each time. It was a lot more comfortable, too.

An icy tingling started to spread through her body. Her toes and fingers felt like they were being jabbed by thousands of tiny needles. Her feet and wrists, arms and legs quickly followed. She could no longer hear her own breathing in the confined space. Her auditory nerves were dead, completely blocked.

Soon she felt nothing, heard nothing. Slowly she slid down that long black tube toward oblivion. Every time she did this she told herself it was only temporary. She never truly believed it. It was just like dying.

Seven of them sat in the room and the lines were clearly drawn. On one side of the table Mother Lei, Mother Che, and Mother Tris sat quietly. Across the table sat Teri, Lan, and Rea. The topsider sat at the head of the table, faceless in his bulky suit. Teri was upset.

"It doesn't make any sense," she said. "How are we supposed to get acclimated to the planet if you keep cutting down on out-time?"

"It's only a temporary measure," said the topsider, his voice flat and lifeless through the suit's speaker.

"That's what you said last time," snapped Teri. "Every month we go out less. It should be the other way around. I don't think any of you know what you're doing."

"Teri, please—" Mother Lei was cut off by a wave of the topsider's hand.

"I'll explain it again," he said. "What we have is basically a methane problem. Frost normally has a certain atmospheric concentration of methane and your metabolism is able to handle that; needs it, in fact. But in the last couple of weeks we've seen a drastic rise in methane all over the planet. It's reached a point where too much exposure to it could be harmful to you. We don't know what's causing it, but we're trying to find out. In the meantime we're attempting to treat it by increasing our methane sinks—places where methane is pulled out of the atmosphere. The problem is that the sinks aren't working rapidly enough. We do know that you shouldn't be exposed to it for long periods of time, so we're reducing the time you spend outside. It's that simple, and only a temporary measure, I assure you."

"That sounds sensible," said Mother Che.

Teri looked at her with disgust. That silly old woman would believe anything they told her. She wasn't able to go outside, anyway. What did she know? What did she care? Teri shook her head and turned back to the topsider.

"This month it's methane. Three months ago it was ammonia. Before that it was something you couldn't even identify. I still say you don't know what you're doing. We're the ones who are going to live on Frost, and we're the ones who ought to be able to decide when we come and go."

"That's clearly impossible," said the topsider. "We have equipment to measure—"

"Stuff your equipment! We know when it's good to go outside and when it's bad. We know how much we can stand, how much we need. Your damn machines just know how to measure our lives. We know how to live them."

She turned to the two siblings who were sitting next to her. "Tell them," she said. "Tell them what I'm saying is the truth."

Lan and Rea sat quietly, eyes downcast. Regardless of what they believed, they were too scared to speak out in the presence of a topsider. The suited ones controlled everything, held all the keys.

"Calm down, Teri," said Mother Lei softly. "They know what's best."

"It's already been decided," said the topsider. "The new schedule will start immediately."

"Damn it, no!" shouted Teri, her eyes flashing with anger around the room. She saw only the gold-tinted faceplate of the topsider and the embarrassed looks of the Mothers and her siblings.

"There will be no further discussion," said the topsider, rising.

"Fools!" shouted Teri, pushing her chair back with a clatter. "You're all a bunch of damn fools and cowards." She turned and ran from the room, her eyes misting over with tears of frustration and disappointment.

Teri ran blindly through the twisted halls and corridors, oblivious to her surroundings. The siblings and Mothers she met either got out of her way or were rudely pushed aside. All she could think of was that the topsiders—a bunch of strangers—were taking her home away from her an hour at a time. They *couldn't* do that. She hit her shoulder rounding a corner, banged a leg in a dark stairwell.

Thirty minutes later Mother Lei finally found her. Teri was curled up in a corner of the observation lounge, her face and both hands pressed against the glass. She was sobbing quietly to herself.

Lei was gentle with her.

Sam watched the readout from Madge's capsule dance across the screen to his far left. He had to strain to see it. Once they entered the wormhole he wouldn't be able to turn his head that much. It didn't matter. Once they dropped inside there was no turning back for any reason, and nothing he could do to speed up the transit time. The readouts from the sleep capsules weren't in his normal field of view simply because there wasn't anything he could do about them once they got underway. If something went wrong it would have to wait. Her vital signs gave a couple of twitches and settled down in the green area. He waited to make sure they had stabilized and then shifted his attention back to the main board.

For a few minutes he just sat there collecting his thoughts and getting everything settled down. If anything was wrong this would be the last time to catch it. A wrinkle in his clothing or a wire brushing his nose could

THE FALL OF WINTER

prove maddening over the length of the trip.
He wouldn't be able to do anything about it.
Pilots had gone over the deep end for less
than that. He took his time and didn't move
until he was satisfied that things were in order.

With his little finger he tapped the code
that let the watchers of the portal know that
he was about to initiate insertion. They flashed
him green.

He acknowledged the transmission and
started the complicated procedure that would
pull them through the twisted fabric of space.
Frost lay at the other end.

"Here we go," he said to himself with a
familiar mixture of controlled fear and anticipation. It didn't feel like dying to him, not at
all.

It was living, living at the limit.

CHAPTER THREE

Sam remembered being eight years old.

He had grown up on Earth far from the noise and frantic excitement of the spaceports, in a rural area that hadn't changed much in the last two hundred years. His father had been a small-scale farmer and Sam's childhood had been quiet. It was years before he dreamed of space.

His parents kept a large wooden kitchen stool outside their back door. It was ancient and weathered, long past its prime. The cats used it for a scratching post, Sam used it for a toy. It managed to survive both.

Sam's favorite game was to climb on top of the stool and tilt forward until it was balanced on its two front legs. It was an eight-year-old kind of thing to do on a lazy afternoon. Then he would rock from side to side and walk the stool across the back yard balanced on the two legs. He often closed his eyes as he went, concentrating on his balance. The sun played warm patterns on his closed eyelids and he seldom fell. He never forgot it.

Balance. The key to the wormholes. It took a special kind of person to be a pilot.

Sam tapped his fingers in a pattern he knew as well as his own name. The real-time readout at the bottom of his field of vision started to shift. He was maneuvering the ship into the proper alignment for insertion. Lights danced in familiar and regular patterns in front of his eyes. He felt the knot in his gut start to loosen a little as the trace of nervousness left his system. Chemicals. The ship was adjusting his metabolism, keeping him safe so that he could keep the ship safe. It was self-preservation —ingrained in him, programmed in the ship.

It took Sam almost a half hour to get himself lined up. The *Kodiak Bear* was built for a different kind of transit and didn't move very well in normal space. The real-time readout flashed green. Everything was set.

A few more taps of Sam's fingers moved the ship past the invisible line that marked the edge of the wormhole's field. Once the wormhole grabbed you there was no backing out. You fell through and fought it all the way. Either you made it or you didn't. It was that simple. It all depended on the pilot.

No matter how many times Sam had gone through this, he still felt apprehensive when he was perched on the edge. He tapped his fingers once more and the bottom fell out.

They were inside the wormhole.

Immediately the ship started resonating. Vibrations came in waves, building one on another, as the *Kodiak Bear* responded to the immense forces tearing at it. Sam knew the ship was filled with a shrieking roar that would continue without pause for the duration of transit time, but he felt it only as vibrations, carefully dampened by the chair he sat in.

Sam was no longer nervous. He was far too busy for that. His attention was riveted to the gauges and computer projections in front of him. The fields of the two plasma accelerators needed constant adjustments to compensate for the ever-shifting dynamics of the wormhole. Even the vibrations provided information as to the status and position of the ship. He made critical decisions at the rate of about thirty per minute and they all had to be right. There was no room for error.

He was busy and he enjoyed it. This was what he lived for. During transit he and the ship were one, extensions of each other. Sometimes the whole was more than the sum of the parts. At times like this he felt larger than life, more than human.

The whole idea of traveling through the wormhole and surviving was balance. The wormhole exerted pressures on the ship and the pilot counteracted them in a continous struggle. It was like driving down the side of a mountain at night with your lights off and your eyes closed.

This intense concentration made it impossible to use temporarily deafened people as pilots. When Sam was wired into the ship he used all his senses—as well as the ship's senses. He was running on the ragged edge, taking in absolutely all the information available to him in order to make split-second decisions. The unconscious effort to even *try* to hear something would be enough to fatally distract him.

Sam took the ship through a particularly complicated maneuver and a smile flashed across his face for a split second. He loved it. But at the same time it was hard work, seemingly endless while it lasted.

He stole a tenth of a second and flicked his eyes to look at the transit clock. Only two minutes had passed since they'd entered the wormhole. Already it seemed like days.

CHIMERA

An organism composed of two or more genetically distinct tissues.

or

An artificially produced individual having tissues of several species.

or

Test tube trouble. The lowest form of life, an insult to God and man.

It all depended on what side of the fence you were on, which dictionary you chose to use.

People still remembered Panacea and the things that happened there. It hadn't been so very long ago.

Panacea was one of the first attempts at bioengineering humans to live on another planet. The planet's atmosphere was just a little off Earth-normal and a small correction of a few metabolic pathways would give man the ability to live there without complicated life support systems. It looked like a very minor change for a major advantage.

Genetic engineering had been riding the crest of a long unbroken string of successes. It was one of the main tools that mankind used when it began to carve out its first tentative path away from Earth. Plants had been modified first, made more productive and adaptable. Animals quickly followed, with equal success. Mankind itself had been the next step. The first few attempts came off without a hitch. Then they reached for Panacea.

From the start it looked just like the others, no problems at all. A thousand tests were run, the results analyzed to five decimal places. It couldn't have looked any better. Chimeras moved onto Panacea full of hopes and dreams for the new planet, unaware of the black disease they carried locked deep inside them.

The disease didn't show up for five generations—a neurological disorder hidden in the complexities of their genetic makeup. Suddenly, the entire population of the planet acted as though it had been drugged. They became irrational, behaved strangely. Their confused distrust of each other became paranoia. Anger became violence. More violence followed.

They turned on themselves. The fifth generation abandoned the new cities and gathered in small bands to attack other small bands. The civilization they had brought with them and built upon quickly fell apart. By the sixth generation, even the bands had disintegrated.

It was every man for himself. There was no seventh generation.

The planet was abandoned, allowed to go on its own path without interference from man. Already the small cities that had been built were crumbling into the jungle. Panacea would forever stand, both in its physical presence and in the minds of men, as a hollow monument to the horror man was capable of producing.

The scientists said it could never happen again. Some people didn't believe them. Even as years passed and there were no more mistakes, they refused to be convinced. Many felt that man should not tamper with man. The Church of the One True Way represented much of that feeling.

And they, too, were looking at Frost.

Morris Twelve knelt at the altar as the evening sun of Paragon streamed through the towering windows of stained glass. The windows were of the highest quality, imported from Earth, handmade by Earth craftsmen. It was quiet in the sanctuary, with the gentle hum of the piped-in prayers a familiar and reassuring background music in his ears. He came at least four times a day, as did all members of the congregation, more on high holy days. At the top of the altar a multifaceted mirrored structure slowly rotated. It represented man; the One True Way, the Only Way, the Ultimate Pilgrim. Morris was alone, or thought he was, and as he knelt the structure reflected the light from the windows and played soft colored bands across his face, across his closed eyes. He was at peace, as much peace as he ever knew.

Morris was a true believer in every sense of the term. He accepted the church's doctrine as his own. It was easier than thinking everything through. He saved what thinking he was capable of for his job. He worked at the spaceport on a welding crew.

He was a simple man, with simple wants and uncomplicated desires. His life had always been that way.

The product of a terminated short-contract marriage, Morris had been raised by the government of Paragon. At age twelve he left the creche and pledged himself to the mechanics guild, the only one that would even consider his application. He was trained as a welder and would die a welder unless he petitioned for reassessment, something he would never consider. Morris was not an ambitious man.

Every day in Morris's life was exactly like every other day. He welded seams on the giant ships in the spaceport and went to church several times a day. On days when he didn't work, he spent most of his time alone in the meditation chambers.

The church of the One True Way was a blessing to him. It made most of his decisions and provided a stable background to hang his life on. Nothing but the church interested him much. The spacecraft he worked on held no magic; they were just hunks of metal to be welded. Space travel itself meant nothing to Morris. He had been born on Paragon and had no desire to go anyplace else. He was happy where he was. Life was good. He had his work and he had his church. Nothing else mattered much.

Morris opened his eyes and shifted his weight. The room was familiar and comforting. Stable. His mind at rest, he closed his eyes again and let his thoughts drift away, guided by the piped-in prayers.

The priest watched him from the shadows, drawing his black cloak tighter around him. He needed two more people for the project. Morris Twelve would do fine. The bootleg copy of his personality profile showed a ninety-nine percentile ranking in his dedication to the church. It also indicated that he had little or no imagination and rarely showed initiative. He was a good worker and did exactly what he was told without a lot of questions. He would fit in nicely.

The profile search had cost plenty. Tapping into Psychotherapy's computer net was expensive and somewhat risky. It was also necessary. They couldn't afford to make a wrong choice at the beginning. The expense was a minor one in the overall operation. Money was one thing the church had plenty of—that and power.

"Pilgrim Twelve," said the priest softly, stepping from the shadows at the rear of the room.

Morris looked around, startled. He stood, confused, and when he saw the priest he bowed from the waist, touching his forehead with his index finger.

"Good evening, Pilgrim," said the priest.

"Man is the spirit and the body of man," began Morris. "He is the Ultimate Manifestation, the Only. We of the flesh—" The priest cut off his litany with a wave of his hand.

"Enough," he said, and Morris visibly relaxed. "I'd like to talk with you if you can spare the time."

The time? A pilgrim always had time for his priest. Morris followed the hooded figure to the rectory, a small room set off to one side of the altar.

The room was wood-paneled, windowless, roughly furnished with a simple desk and two straight-backed chairs. The Ten Great Points of Man were listed on a scroll mounted on one wall. As they sat the priest slid back his hood, an indication of informality.

"You have worked well for the church," said the priest, offering Morris a weedstick. He took it even though he didn't usually indulge. Who could refuse a priest? He scratched the lightspot with his fingernail and inhaled deeply.

"Thank you, lord," he said, suppressing a cough. "I've always tried my best to serve." It was true, he felt. He had always surpassed his recruitment quota, and for the last five years had tithed twenty percent of his wages to the church, twice the required amount.

"It has not gone unnoticed," said the priest. "On the contrary, we have been watching you closely. We feel you have the call."

Morris choked. "The . . . the call?" He shook his head to clear his thoughts. Weed always made him dizzy. He didn't like it.

"The church has a job for you, a secular one. It's quite important."

"I'll try my best," said Morris, confused. He'd never been asked to do anything out of the ordinary before.

"Are you free to leave your job for a brief period on church business?" The priest already knew the answer to that, as he knew almost everything about Morris Twelve. The background sheets had been most comprehensive.

"My employment contract has the usual religious obligation clause. I'm at your disposal."

Typical, thought the priest. *Such blind obedience that he doesn't even ask me what we want him to do. He'd probably kill his sister if the church asked him. Sheep, they're all sheep.*

"Have you ever heard of a planet called Frost?" asked the priest.

Morris shook his head. He seemed to recall there was something about it in the news a few years ago, but he couldn't remember what it was exactly. Morris didn't pay much attention to the news. It was always too unsettling.

"Something . . ." He shook his head. "I can't remember."

"Terraforming operation," said the priest.

Morris nodded eagerly. He knew what that meant.

"Chimeras," said the priest, drawing the word out to its last bitter syllable.

Morris snapped back in his chair as if he'd been hit in the face. Reflexively he pointed to his forehead and slapped his open palm against his chest: *I man*. Horror grew in his eyes. The priest nodded slowly.

"I find it as unthinkable as you do," he said. "That is why the church is going to try to stop it. That is why the church needs you."

"Me?" Morris trembled. Chimeras!

The priest leaned back in his chair. "The church has applied for and received an official certificate to lobby in support of our cause. We'll be sending a delegation to Frost shortly to express our views and I want you to be one of the group. As an officer of the church, I will head the delegation."

"But what can I do there?" asked Morris. "I'm just a welder. I have no education, no skills."

"You have one of the greatest qualifications of all," said the priest. "You believe in our cause. You believe in the church and its teachings."

Morris touched himself again: head, chest. That much was true. He did believe. The priest did not choose to mention that, by law, they were required to send along a certain number of laymen for each church official.

"Your job will be to create noise, to keep our position in front of those who are working there. You will spread the word of our faith among their workers, perhaps even convert some of them. You can do that, can't you?"

"Of course, lord. I can try."

"You may also be called upon to—uh—perform certain disruptive acts, if you know what I mean. Anything that serves to slow or stop the spread of the nonhuman chimeras is in the best interests of the church. You can do that, too?"

"Of course, lord."

The priest stood, flipped his hood back up.

"Good," he said. "We understand each other. You should get your affairs in order as soon as possible. There will be a meeting tonight after evening services. I expect you there. We leave in two days."

Morris rose, touched his forehead, and bowed. "Thank you, lord," he said with feeling. "It is my pleasure to serve you and the church." He turned and left the room.

The priest exhaled deeply and threw his cloak over the back of his chair. With the touch of a concealed button one wall slid back, revealing an unbroken view of the city streets two stories below. He hated being closed up in the tiny room. He hated many other things about the priesthood, but there were occasional compensations. He lit another weed stick and stared out the window.

The priest arrived early and filled up his tray. He walked across the crowded public cafeteria and found an empty booth in back. The large room was incredibly noisy, a perfect place for their meeting. With so much background clatter no one could possibly overhear their conversation. Nick had set it up that way. Nick set everything up.

Sitting down, the priest started eating. He ate mechanically, showing no interest in the amorphous food he'd piled on his tray. It was simply fuel for the body, nothing more. He wondered how much money Nick would have for him today. The potatoes were cold.

He'd almost finished when Nick sat down across from him, sliding his tray onto the table. He was wearing an ordinary gray robe and his face was covered, as usual, by a skintex mask of the type favored by members of the Fuller cult. He wore the mask not for religious reasons, but to hide his identity. For the same reason, he spoke through a voice modulator and was wearing gloves. Nick never took chances.

"You got the people," he said. It was not a question, but a statement. The modulator gave his voice a slight echo.

The priest nodded.

"This is the last time I'll see you before you leave. I want you to understand how clean this has to be."

"The church has legitimate business on Frost," said the priest. "It's a good cover for what you want. There shouldn't be any problem."

"There *won't* be any problem," snapped Nick, "or it'll be you who'll pay the price. Do I make myself clear?"

The priest flinched. Extortion, drugs, smuggling—Nick had evidence linking him to that and more. What he had on Nick was nothing. He didn't even know who he worked for. Whoever it was had a lot of power. Doors had opened for the priest since he'd met Nick and there'd always been plenty of money.

"The terraforming efforts on Frost must fail," said Nick, his mask hiding any expression. "Use whatever methods that seem appropriate to block them."

The priest leaned back in the booth. "If the Bishop knew what my real reasons for this trip were, he'd kill me. He thinks this is a straightforward lobbying effort."

"The Bishop won't find out unless you fail. If that happens, he'll be the least of your worries."

That much the priest understood all too well. An immense amount of money was at stake here, and even more important than the money was the power. Whoever controlled Frost also controlled the phase-shift point. They would not be happy if he failed.

Nick handed him a thick envelope. "Here's something for your expenses," he said. "An additional sum has been added to your private account with us. There will be more when you return."

The priest resisted the impulse to open the envelope. It felt like a lot. He put it carefully away in a deep pocket.

"You must be careful," said Nick, standing up. "More than that, you must be successful."

"You can count on me," said the priest.

Nick stared at him for a long moment, causing the priest to shift uncomfortably in the booth. Then he waved his hand at his untouched tray. "I don't see how you can eat this garbage," he said. He turned and left, walking easily toward the exit.

The priest watched him go and wondered once more who the man's bosses were. It could be a government agency from one of a number of planets or it could be a rival corporation. Frost was caught in the middle of a power struggle and he wasn't even clear about who was fighting. Wars had started over less. But the reasons didn't really concern him—only the money was important.

He shrugged to himself and patted the envelope. Sliding his empty tray aside, he pulled Nick's in front of him. He ate mechanically.

Sam felt the twists and tugs of the energy fields as if they were acting on his bare body. He was that much in tune with the ship and its sensors. Sidepaths in the wormhole, most of them uncharted, grabbed him with a sinking feeling in the pit of his stomach, a falling sensation. He ignored most of them and fought the nausea as he passed them by. Once in a while, as his course indicated, he switched down one or another of the sidepaths. It was a wrenching feeling, compounded by immense strains on the ship.

He was dead tired and knew it. The realtime clock indicated almost eighty hours had passed. Eighty hours of split-second decisions, of constant alertness. He was running on the ragged edge now, at the limit of the ability of the ship to keep him going. His body felt drained of energy in spite of the chemicals coursing through his bloodstream. His mouth was dry, his eyes burned. Maybe they should have done it in two jumps rather than trying it all at once. But that would have meant a delay in the middle, a forced rest period. It was also, to some extent, a matter of pride. No pilot liked to take two jumps when he could do it in one. It was a sign of weakness.

The end was in sight, just a little bit farther.

At this point, time and distance meant little to Sam. He felt them both as rhythm and pacing rather than something that could be measured. He couldn't *see* the end, nor could he measure the exact distance, but like a skilled freeball player who always knew where he was on the court without looking, Sam *felt* the exit with a sureness that was beyond measure.

Then he was out.

It was a sudden, abrupt transition. Warped time became real time in the blinking of an eye. Sam felt a moment of sheer panic, as if he were about to go careening through the planetary system. He was so geared to the rapid time frame in the wormhole, it took him a few seconds to make the mental adjustment and realize that he would exit the wormhole with exactly the same speed with which he entered it. Nearly zero.

The ship hung essentially motionless in space. The board in front of him flashed in code, indicating that the welcoming committee had spotted them. Pickup in twenty minutes. He removed one finger from its sheath and pressed an outside button that activated the retrieval system in the pods for Madge and Roger.

Madge came out first and went right to Sam. Frost was a vague disk in the viewscreen. It was closer to the phase-shift point than most planets were, but still a good day's travel away. The sun looked brighter than she'd expected. Working quickly, she started to extricate Sam from his complicated harness.

As Madge removed the last metabolic support tube, she walked around in front of him.

"How're you doing?" she signed. "You feel okay?"

Sam managed a shaky grin and slumped forward, dead to the world.

He slept all the way to Frost.

CHAPTER FOUR

The topsider called Henry Sokol sat across the low table from Teri. Mother Lei was at her left. The lights in the conference room were dim. Teri tried to look into the eyes of the man in front of her but couldn't see past the gold-tinted lenses in his suit. She was ready for her punishment, whatever it was. She didn't know which of her many sins she was being punished for, but it really didn't matter. Her sins were all the same, they came from the rebellion she felt against the people who kept her from her planet.

"Teri, listen to him," said Mother Lei. "He knows what's best."

Teri shook her head and bit the edge of her tongue to try to control her anger. Topsiders always thought they knew everything, but they knew nothing, nothing at all. They couldn't even walk around without those silly suits, so how could they possibly know what Frost was like?

Teri had never seen a topsider without his suit on. Maybe they were monsters, who could tell? To her they were just something to be avoided. Their voices sounded the same through their speaker grills. They certainly all looked the same in their bulky white suits with mirrors for eyes, speakers for mouths, twin tubes for noses that curled around to the boxes on their backs that they could not live without. She felt they looked less human than she did, whatever "human" meant.

"What am I being punished for this time?" asked Teri impatiently. "What ironclad rule did I break?"

"No, Teri," said Mother Lei. "There's no need for that attitude."

Teri looked at her mother, painfully aware of the gulf between them. It was a gulf built on more than the years that separated them, more than their biological differences. It was almost as though they were from different worlds, and in a sense they were.

Lei's world was one of walls, ceilings, floors. Teri could not understand how the Mothers tolerated such conditions, much less preferred them. Her world was open sky, rivers, mountains, oceans. It was a basic conflict between them, one they had never managed to resolve.

"I never said you were going to be punished, Teri," said the topsider.

"You didn't have to say it. I always am when I'm brought here."

"Always is a pretty strong word, Teri. Maybe this time will be different."

"*Fluffer drops*," said Teri under her breath.

"Show some respect, child," said Mother Lei, shocked. "When will you ever learn to control your tongue?"

"Never, I hope," snapped Teri. "I'm not like you, always doing what other people think is best."

"When other people know better, I listen."

"That's all you ever do is listen," said Teri. "You never *think*."

Mother Lei sighed, feeling very tired. It seemed like all they ever did was fight, and for no good reason at all. Maybe someday Teri would understand why she felt the way she did. After all, her daughter was still young.

Maybe that was the problem. Youth.

Her hands were trembling in her lap. If this went on, they would only fight. It could serve no purpose. She looked away from Teri and faced the topsider.

"Mr. Sokol, I don't feel well." She rose from her seat. "If you don't mind, I think I'll leave."

"Certainly, Lei," he said. "I'll catch up with you later."

As the older woman left the room, Teri relaxed. She could never understand why they always argued.

The topsider stared at Teri through his golden mirrors. "She is what she has to be, you know," he said. "In that way she's no different from you."

Teri looked up, confused. This didn't sound like punishment, more like a lecture. "What do you mean?" she asked.

"Mother Lei and her sisters are products of their upbringing, a carefully controlled mixture of heredity and environment. Mother Lei could no more think like you do than she could fly. Her attitudes are fixed. They were meant to be that way."

"I don't understand."

"From one point of view the Mothers could be considered simply a way to bring your generation into existence. It's hardly fair, I know, but you could say that that was their primary function. It's reasonable to assume we'd like them to have certain attitudes, and they do. It makes our job easier."

"I'll bet," said Teri. "You topsiders try to manipulate everything."

"Don't be so hard on us, Teri. We have jobs to do just like everyone else."

"Some job you have, laying down a bunch of stupid rules and regulations."

"We expect that attitude from you. I'd be surprised if you felt differently."

"Me?"

"All of you. Don't you see that you and your siblings have been shaped as surely as the Mothers and their Mothers before them? It's all very carefully planned."

Teri laughed. "A generation of troublemakers doesn't sound like very careful planning to me. I think you blew it."

"Do you suppose we'd rather have a bunch of mindless docile people unable to think for themselves? That's not very good stock to populate a planet with."

"It sounds like you're talking about animals, not people."

"Sometimes it looks that way. It has to. We need people who will be able to go out and tame this planet, live on it, make it their own. That takes a very special kind of person. We've done everything we can to make your generation fit that mold. Your early training was manipulated as surely as your genetic structure, and for exactly the same purpose. If Frost is ever going to be populated, it will have to be by people like yourself."

"Rebellious pioneers," said Teri sarcastically, still unconvinced. "Somehow breeding a bunch of malcontents just doesn't sound like the best way to go about this."

"It's worked before on other planets," said Sokol. "And it ought to work here. We're counting on it. Our studies show that this method has the best chance for success. We expect you to rebel against your elders, against us. It's normal for you to question our rules, to dislike everything we do. We expect you to be constantly dissatisfied. It's all part of the plan, and the end result of the plan is to conquer Frost."

"Why tell me all this?"

"Because you're a born leader, Teri, and

you always have been. I could quote your psych profiles from age two, but you'd probably be offended. It's clear to us that you are going to be one of the central forces among the first generation out on Frost, so we thought you ought to have a better idea about what we've been doing."

"Building troublemakers. Did you expect them all to be as stubborn as me?"

The topsider laughed, but the distorted sound that came from his speaker was a gross parody of laughter. It sounded more like the rasping shriek of a file against steel.

"Not quite *that* stubborn," he said. "But you're a special case. We make allowances."

"Thanks for nothing."

"Teri, you've got to understand that we expect resentment from you. In fact, it's necessary. If you were satisfied with the way things were—like Mother Lei and her kind—you would never want to leave the dome to start with, much less face the hardships of a hostile planet." He paused, tapped his fingers against the arm of his chair. "This was all worked out over two hundred years ago, long before I was born," he said reflectively. "Your generation is just the end of one stage and the beginning of another."

Teri looked at him, trying and failing to read any expression into his mechanical voice, his awkward body posture. It sounded like he was telling the truth, but she wasn't convinced. They were alway tricking her, trying to make her do what they wanted. Why should this man be any different.

"The rules, then," she said. "If what you're saying is the truth, some of the rules must be there simply to frustrate us, make us mad."

"True."

"Then what about the rules for outside time? Is that one of the things you manipulate just to get us upset?"

He shook his head. "I'm afraid not. There are serious problems, believe me."

Teri slapped the table in anger. "The same old story," she shouted, the small hairs on her face bristling. "You topsiders lie so much we can never tell when you're telling the truth. We *can* go outside more, I just know we can. We *have* to. There must be a way."

He waited for Teri to calm down.

"There are ways," he said quietly, evenly. "But you wouldn't like them."

"Try me," she snapped, her chin jutting out.

"Some of our scientists think a detoxification program might help, but just for short periods of time. It would be like the one you have now to get rid of the poisons you pick up in the dome, but it would be more intensive. It would be more painful, too, and only a very temporary solution. At most it would buy you a few more hours at a time."

A few more hours! Anything!

"I'll do it," she said without hesitation. "And so will the others."

"Not so fast," he said. "I'll have to talk it over with the rest of the staff and see what they think. It might be a good idea. At any rate, I'll get back to you as soon as a decision is made." He motioned to the door. The interview was over.

Teri started to leave, stopped, turned back to him.

"Is that a promise or more fluff drops?"

"It's a promise, Teri. I'll do my best."

She left the room, wanting to believe him, but not quite being able to.

Sokol rose from his chair, stood in the middle of the empty room. With his tongue, he flipped a switch inside his helmet, locking into a secure, confidential channel.

"Did you get all that?" he asked.

"Yes." The voice was clear in his earplug.

"What do you think?"

"She's the one, all right. Give her some elbow room, but watch her closely. You know what we want."

"I understand," he said. He knew only too well what they wanted. They wanted everything.

Mother Lei sat cross-legged on the cot in her small room, separated from the similar cubicles of her sisters by flimsy movable partitions that served as walls. Although she could hear their muted voices, she felt miles away from them, lost in her own thoughts. She stretched her legs out, feeling very much alone, and reached down to open the locker at the foot of her cot.

Most of her possessions were meaningless,

trivial, without character. Her personal items were no different from those of any other Mother. They all wore the same drab clothes that were replaced by the topsiders when they got too frayed. Everything they had was as interchangeable as they themselves were—the walls, the clothes, the food. There were few places for individuality in their enclosed and orderly world. Mother Lei looked carefully through her locker, removing folded clothes and stacking them neatly beside her until she found the beads.

Her strand was a little more than a meter long, passed down to her by her Mothers from their Mothers. She had added three beads to the strand herself.

They called them birth beads, small spheres carved out of bits of discarded plastic. Some of the beads were plain, others were covered with complex designs; it all depended on the Mother who had done the work. As surely as any calendar, they marked the passing of time. As surely as any cry for help, they spoke of a desire to be treated as more than objects to be manipulated. Mother Lei held the history of her race in her hands and spread it carefully out on the cot.

She ran her fingers lightly over the beads and stopped at Teri's. It rattled slightly as the four balls carved from the same block of plastic, one inside the other, slid around. It had taken her a long time to make this bead. It was special. Teri had always been special.

Mother Lei had started with a scrap of black

plastic and carved it down to size, shaped it
into a sphere. That had been the easy part.
She had carried it around with her for the
next two weeks, taking it out and holding it,
touching it, waiting for the design to grow in
her mind as the implanted embryo grew inside her.

She carved the surface with a filigreed pattern two millimeters deep, working four windows into the intricate lines. It looked like a
round, black snowflake. Next she worked
through the windows to form a ball within
the outer ball. It was hard work, delicate,
exacting. She had to free the inner ball without harming the outer one. It took six weeks,
but she didn't begrudge the time she'd spent.
Time was one thing she had plenty of back
then.

After the inner ball was free of the outer
ball, she embellished it like the first one. Then
she cut through to work on another ball within
the second. That was harder—the spaces she
had to work through were very small. It took
her two months to free it, another month to
decorate it to her satisfaction.

The last ball was the hardest of all. Lining
up the holes in the outer shells, she had almost no room to work through. Yet this was
the most important one, the center, the core,
the spirit. She had to steal a fine probe from
a topsider's tool box to even reach the inner
surface. When she finally freed it, she polished it with a passion. By the time she
finished, it hung suspended within the delicate

outer shells like a precious jewel. Teri was born the next week.

Some of the other beads on the strand showed similar care and dedication; others were stark in their simplicity, some almost gaudy. But they all said the same thing: this birth is important to me.

Most of the Mothers would never know the children they bore. Separated at birth, the children had more to do with topsiders than their own flesh and blood. The beads were a connection, a bridge between the generations. It would soon be lost.

Although the topsiders gave them trivial things to do once in a while, the Mothers always had time on their hands. It weighed heavily on them and they filled it with small rituals as best they could, but they could never escape the fact that their main purpose in life was to produce the next link in the chain that would lead to the population of Frost. Teri's generation would have no time for such rituals as the birth beads. They would be too busy carving out a new life on a new planet. What was left of the old ways would disappear, be gone forever.

Mother Lei looked at the beads, stroked them lightly again. She looked at the one that was hers, the one her Mother had carved. It was light green, circled with deep ridges. She had barely known her real mother, but she could touch this bead and feel her mother's spirit through it. The beads spoke with silent voices, and it saddened her to think that soon no one would care to listen.

As she packed away the strand of beads her heart was filled with a sense of almost unbearable loss.

Roger was grumpy. He always felt that way for a couple of days after phase-shift. It would have been a simple thing to have Madge fix him up, tweak his metabolism a little bit, but he didn't ask her. Sometimes it was a definite advantage to be a little grumpy. People didn't try to mess with you as much. He walked down the hall of the orbiting station, the soles of his shoes squeaking on the polished floor as he headed for the conference room and the waiting committee.

He was the last to arrive. Some of the others he knew from the time he had worked with the Paragon group before, some he didn't. The meeting room was large, well appointed. They sat around a real wood table; a wall-sized port was currently opaqued. It all spelled money.

Jud Walsh, the administrator, stood as he entered. "Hello, Roger," he said. "Good to see you again." He had met their ship when it docked at the station.

Roger nodded, ignored the extended hand. He walked to the head of the table and took the only vacant chair. It was a mixed group: young and old, men and women. They all looked very serious.

"From the information you sent me, it looks

like you have a pretty sticky problem. It would have to be, or you wouldn't have called me in on this." Roger looked at Walsh. "I purposely put a high price tag on the option clause hoping you wouldn't pick it up. You did, so it's obviously big trouble. I've seen the data and I agree, but give it to me in plain words. Sometimes that helps to give me a better picture."

Walsh waved his hand at the person sitting directly across from him. "This is Dr. Mulhauser, head of the physical science coordination committee. All this has been his headache for quite some time. Suppose we let him brief you. Fred?"

Dr. Mulhauser was a thin, nervous-looking man with closely cropped white hair, a sparse brown mustache for contrast. With a quick, darting glance in Roger's direction, he adjusted his wire-rimmed glasses and shuffled the computer flimsies in front of him. Roger eyed him warily. Glasses were a rarity these days, a sure sign of vanity. There were very few vision problems that couldn't be easily corrected. The man coughed, cleared his throat.

"Basically, Mr. Trent, what we have on Frost is a constantly recurring atmospheric problem that manifests itself in a variety of different ways, none of which are very clear to us. The nitrogen concentration of the planet's atmosphere fluctuates wildly, much more than our projective models can account for. Particularly, we get a lot of nasty ammonia compounds we'd rather not have. But that's only one side of a many-sided problem. Frost's methane level is far too high and we can't seem to bring it down. We've tried all kinds of sink systems, but nothing seems to have much of an effect. Every time we initiate a reduction procedure something happens and more is pumped into the system. We end up with more than we started out with and I'll be damned if we can figure out where it's all coming from. By our calculations methane shouldn't even be out there at all in any amount significantly above trace levels."

He flipped through the flimsies and pulled one out, scanned it quickly.

"By far the biggest stumbling block in the way of the project are the damn organics," he said, waving the flimsy at Roger. "Look at this: widespread dissemination of complex organic macromolecules, usually poisonous. Some of them tie up oxygen at a fearsome rate. They'll pop up without warning simultaneously all over the planet. When we control one it just seems to drop off and pretty soon another one crops up. We can't even hold our own against them."

"What control systems are you using?" asked Roger.

"You're familiar with SR-50?"

"Of course."

"A nice little strain of plankton, highly adaptable, easily manipulated. We use it a lot as a substrate for our P-9 bacterial colonies. A damn good nitrogen fixer, just sucks it right out of the atmosphere. We have—let me see—eighty-seven rafts in the ocean, ranging in size from one hundred to one thousand square kilometers. All the major lakes and most of the minor ones have been seeded with it. Pulls out one hell of a lot of nitrogen, but we're always behind." He looked up at Roger, shook his head.

"The planet pumps out *that* much, can you imagine? Mutant strains of P-9 have a forty-six-hour turnover per hundred square kilometers, so we can tailor them to pull out the organics, but that's forty-six hours *after* we've identified the new organic *and* developed the mutant strain of P-9 to handle it. That's too much lag time, way too much, especially with bioforms on the surface."

"I'm going to put you on the spot, Dr. Mulhauser," said Roger. "Would you say that these reactions are native to Frost or the result of the terraforming operation?"

"That's hard to say. My first guess would be that they are native reactions, inherent to the planet, but I couldn't say that for sure. We've done so many things here that any byproducts of our activities would be difficult to pinpoint at this stage." He paused, rubbed his chin thoughtfully. "It might be possible, I guess, but it would be a mess to untangle."

"What about the native biomass?" asked Roger. "In general, what does it consist of?"

"Very few life forms managed to survive the initial procedures, as you would expect. Most of them are primitive, insects and the like. A few more advanced species are quite hardy, surprisingly resilient and adaptable, though most of them fall outside my area of concern. There are some interesting deep-sea forms— mostly sulfide based—some lichens, the trees, and, of course, the fluffers. Dr. Brooker could tell you more about them." He looked to the man on his left.

Roger knew Dr. Brooker from the last time around with this group and didn't have much respect for the man. He was devious and a sloppy worker. A stupid oversight on his part had cost Roger an extra week's work on Faith.

"What about the fluffers, Don?" asked Roger.

"Interesting creatures, though extremely primitive," said Dr. Brooker. "We've studied thousands of them, but have come up with more unanswered questions than facts. They're warm-blooded egg-layers, diurnal, have simple digestive and reproductive systems. Their metabolism, on the other hand, is quite complex."

"Sentient?" asked Roger with a wry smile.

Dr. Brooker drew himself up straight, glared at Roger. "Of course not," he said haughtily. "That's simply not possible. We ruled that out completely, long before we committed ourselves to the project."

Roger hadn't expected him to say anything different. He was a company man all the way down the line. Unity had far too much invested to admit that the possibility even existed.

"Are you sure?" he asked.

"Certainly," he said firmly. "Beyond a doubt."

Roger noticed several people shifting nervously in their chairs around the table. It was obviously a very sensitive area.

"Others don't think so," he said.

"Others are fools, dreamers. They think anything that walks upright and uses its hands is a rational creature. That's stupid, plain and simple. They see what they want to see, not what's there. I've looked at a hell of a lot more of the damn things than they have and I've never seen anything that would even suggest that they have any intelligence beyond that of a moderately brain-damaged rat."

Roger turned back to Dr. Mulhauser. "What about the sulfides? You seem to have an excess of them. Does that pose any problems?"

"Some," he admitted. "Not too much, though. The atmosphere will always be a little acidic, but we've planned for that."

"But you haven't planned for the acid rains, have you?" asked Roger.

"No. Not to the degree that we have now. That's another facet to the overall problem, but one that we are confident we can overcome once we get a handle on the other difficulties."

Roger leaned back in his chair, took a piece of paper from his tunic, and passed it to Walsh.

"These are the types of people I'd like to talk to right away. Set up appointments for them to see me one at a time for the next couple of days. I'll be roaming around the installation some, too. There'll be other people I want to see before I go down to the surface. I'll have to have free reign."

"You've got it," said Walsh, taking Roger's list and scanning it quickly. It was a mixed bag of people, from maintenance personnel to project coordinators. Why the hell would he want to talk to a microwave technician, a cook? He couldn't fathom how Roger worked, but somehow he usually pulled it all together. He was the best.

"This is your baby, Roger. Just let us know what you need."

"I'll do that," said Roger.

Teri clung to her seat on the floater as the rough ground rushed by a few meters below them. Her ear flaps were closed tightly and her eyes were slits against the howling wind. It was cold, but the cold never seemed to bother her. She felt the wind much more than the temperature. The screen up front did little more than shield the driver, not that he needed it. He was a topsider, dressed in one of their ugly, bulky suits.

She tried to take everything in at once, but it was impossible. There was simply too much to see, most of it new to her. In all her life she had never been out of sight of the dome except for one or two short trips with the topsiders. The expanse and variety of the planet took her breath away.

It was stark country for the most part, yet somehow beautiful. They passed over thousands of square kilometers of harsh tundra, a low, flat area full of scrubby plants and interlocking rivers. To Lan it looked foreboding and desolate, but not to Teri, sitting beside him. In the gnarled bushes twisted by the bitter wind, she saw life. It was all in your point of view.

Later they skimmed low over a flooded marsh. The reeds and grasses were covered by a thin layer of ice. It would melt by noon, but for now it seemed like a frosted sculpture made of the finest crystal. It was the most delicate and fragile thing Teri had ever seen. It held her attention as they passed by and captured her imagination for much longer than that.

"Almost there," said the topsider as the floater dipped sharply to the left. His words, garbled by the small speaker in his suit, were nearly whipped away by the wind. Teri gripped her seat rail tighter in spite of being strapped in, and leaned into the turn. The wind whipped her fur and she loved it.

The floater skirted a large rock outcropping and swung into a protected cove. The base was in rough country where the mountain range met the sea with abrupt cliffs of cascading rock and ice. A scattering of small buildings and crates of equipment sat in a cleared area. They landed in the middle and another suited figure came to meet them.

This place was currently being used as a temporary base by the topsiders, but eventually it would be home to many of Teri's people. There were other installations like it scattered around the planet. Each would hold an initial population of two or three hundred. They'd have plenty of room to grow, to expand.

Teri looked at the mountains with awe. They towered far above everything, snow-capped, rugged. After so much time cooped up in the stifling confines of the dome, she had a little trouble adjusting to the open country around her. So much land!

The suited figures led Teri's group off to one of the buildings. It was time for the first detox treatment. For every six hours they spent outside on Frost they had to undergo twenty minutes of detoxification. For once, the top-siders hadn't lied. They were going to give it a chance.

The detoxification procedure was involved and fairly painful. Basically a filtration system, their lungs and liver had to be cleansed, scrubbed. The poisons had to be removed from their bloodstream. It was only a temporary solution and six hours later it had to be repeated.

As she stood outside the building waiting her turn, Teri watched the wind blow fine snow from a nearby mountain peak. She felt the earth under her feet, the breeze in her fur. The cold air smelled good, clean, with a trace of the sea. A shiver ran through her body, but it wasn't from the temperature. It was the shiver of anticipation, of excitement. She wanted Frost.

No price was too great to pay for that.

CHAPTER FIVE

They wanted the stars and they paid the price. Their rewards were huge, but for the men and women who piloted the ships the price was steep: a world without sound.

Sam remembered the day the music died for him. He remembered it as clearly as yesterday. It happened to all pilots and no matter how much they prepared for that day it came all too suddenly. When the curtain of silence fell, it fell with an unheard crash and it fell forever.

For the last two months of training, Sam, as well as the other prospective pilots, wore earplugs whenever they weren't in classes. It was a convenient form of deafness, a temporary one they could manipulate by removing the plugs. They spoke only in sign language and tried to learn the habits and rituals of pilots. This was supposed to prepare them for

93

the way the rest of their lives would be, and it failed miserably. For a lifetime of total silence, there could be no adequate preparation.

On Sam's last free weekend he took a tube to the coast, leaving his uniforms and fatigues in his locker. The Cape was crowded as usual, loud and full of activity. That was the last thing he wanted. He went to the Rent/All and punched out for a small electric. The lady at the desk looked at his disheveled appearance and asked for a large deposit and multiple identification papers. His pilot card was all he needed. Her attitude changed abruptly. His electric was ready and waiting before he left the building.

He drove south along the ocean, leaving the base behind. For the first few miles, he was surrounded by tall buildings that blocked out everything. He could be on Broadway in Old York for all the difference it made. Too many people, too many electrics, too much hectic confusion. Bikes overflowed from their lanes and drifted into the traffic slots. Small peds darted in and out, engines whining. People crossed in the middle of traffic, putting entirely too much faith in the autobrake systems. Horns and whistles, shouts and screams surrounded him. Sam reached for his plugs, fingered them a minute, and put them back into his pocket. Hi-rise condos and offices lined the ocean side of the road like a giant fence. He'd driven twenty minutes before he caught his first fleeting glimpse of the water.

It was another half an hour before he left

the clamor behind. The Cape spread more to the west and north than to the south. This area was fragile—palmettos and dunes—constantly reshaped by hurricanes, storms, winds, and tides. He continued driving with no clear destination in mind. He just wanted to get away.

The coastal area was beautiful, essentially untouched, unchanged in hundreds of years. Here and there a solitary house clung to the beach, weathered by years of exposure. Mostly the land was covered with scrub palmettos, dotted here and there with a few stands of pines, often bent away from the beach, their branches and trunks grotesquely twisted by years of yielding to the prevailing winds off the ocean. Sam found a deserted section of beach and pulled the small electric off the road.

He walked up and down the beach for hours, turning shells over with his toes, staring out over the water. The pounding of the surf was a constant, unrelenting roar in his ears. Occasionally a flock of gulls would fly overhead, cackling and cawing. He soaked up the sounds, stored them away for the days when there would be no sounds. A solitary fisherman cast a net into the churning surf. Sam sat on a dune and watched him. Time after time the net came up empty. The man was dark and tanned, his skin leathered by the sun. To Sam's left a small crab clicked across the sand. The sun started to set and the man continued to cast the net, occasionally coming up with a small silver fish which he collected in a white bucket. Between the waves, Sam could hear the splash of the net against the water. It made a flat, slapping sound. That, too, Sam filed away.

As it grew dark, Sam walked back to the electric. He drove further south, away from the Cape, away from his appointment with silence. It was Saturday night. Monday was the day.

He saw the lights first and the lights became windows, orange rectangles that spilled diffused light into the darkness. When he got closer, the outlines of a large structure took shape. Music and laughter, as well as light, broke the dark stillness of the night. There were several electrics parked in a sandy lot. He joined them.

The building had once been a Coast Guard rescue station. It was over two hundred years old and filled with rooms that sprawled and interconnected at odd angles. There were several bars inside, and jiveboxes in almost every room. A wide balcony faced the ocean, a wooden pier cut out beyond the surf.

The decor was eclectic, a hodgepodge mixture heavily weighted toward space and the sea, the two prime activities of the area. A watercolor painting of the first Mars landing hung on one wall, framed by a draped fish net covered with shells and starfish. A vintage Bonstell print of Saturn was matched by a recent holo taken from the same angle. It was hard to tell which was more breathtaking, the dream or the reality. In between the two hung a sketch of the shrimp fleet leaving Sebastian, their hydrofoils skimming proudly in the setting sun. Conversations drifted by, blending with the music from the jiveboxes. Laughter rang from one of the rooms off to the side: a happy place. Sam took a stool at the main bar.

"What'll it be, Spacer?" asked the bartender.

"Is it that obvious?" asked Sam, noticing the man had spoken to him, not signed.

The bartender pointed to Sam's hands. Tattoos marked the places where his crystals would be implanted Monday. The implants were done after the ear operation, all in the same day. A rite of passage, a coming of age.

"Beer," he said.

"What kind?"

"A cold one."

The bartender nodded, cracked the seal on a tall pint of Moonstar and set it in front of him. Sam flipped open his purse and pulled out a bill. The bartender shook his head.

"When are they cutting you?" he asked.

"Monday," said Sam.

"When do you lift?"

"Tuesday."

"Your money's no good here tonight," said the bartender. "Put it in the jive if you want."

The bartender walked down behind the polished bar and took a bill from an overflowing mug, brought it back and slid it in the register slot. Sam understood immediately.

Being a pilot meant you were never alone, never without friends as long as there were other pilots around. They were bound together by the very things that separated them from the rest of society. Deafness cut them off from the majority of the people they met. The loss of hearing and the lives they chose to live gave

pilots more in common than blood relatives.
The mug of bills was always there for pilots
down on their luck or for people like Sam,
almost-pilots walking the Earth like normal
people for the last time. The mug was always
full.

Sam toyed with his beer, listening to the
people around him. Shrimpers, mostly, they
talked of tides and storms, of good times and
bad, of the fantastic catches and the empty
hauls. They talked of their children and of
men long dead. Even with the stars in mankind's hands, the sea could still be a cruel place
to die. They lied, they boasted, they cried, and
they spoke from their hearts. They spoke like
all people, the fabric of their lives a mixture
of truth, hope, and bravado. To hear them
talk, they would spit in the eye of the worst
storm imaginable and go down with a song
on their lips.

It was idle bar talk, the usual pack of lies
that hold more truth than any number of law
books. They were casually overheard conversations, conversations Sam would never overhear again.

In the next room Sam saw a group of pilots
talking. Even from this distance and through
the distracting noise he could read their conversations clearly. This would be his future.
He could join them tonight or not, they would
understand. Knowing this was his last time
out, they wouldn't approach him unless he
wanted them to. Some people liked to be alone
this last time, others didn't. It was a personal
decision and respected as such.

Another Moonstar appeared in front of Sam. He chugged the dregs of the first and picked up the cold one. Pushing away from the stool he walked to the nearest jivebox and scanned the music. He was surprised at how many of the songs he recognized. Ever since he'd been accepted into pilot's training he'd tried to put music behind him, knowing he would lose it forever. Closing the door on something he loved that much had been hard and he hadn't completely succeeded.

Music had always been a large part of his life, an important part. He'd taught himself to play the guitar, banjo, and mandolin. Over the years he'd gotten better and better, playing first for his family, then for friends, and later in front of strangers. After a couple of beers he could even be coaxed into singing, belting out a whisky tenor that sounded far better than he thought.

He hadn't picked up a guitar in years, nor had he sung. After Monday he wouldn't even be able to hear his own voice. He was trying to put these things away, hide them in a place where their loss wouldn't bother him, if there was such a place.

The songs on the jive were songs of the sea, of space, of men facing hostile conditions and surviving. The melodies danced through his head as he read the titles. He could almost smell the salt spray, feel the crush of lift-off. They were real and honest songs, written by people who had lived the lives they sang about. Somehow, it fit this place.

Above the jivebox was a wall cluttered with

poems ranging from obscene limericks to complicated sonnets. Some were written on fine paper, others scrawled on napkins and labels from beer bottles.

A band warmed up in one of the larger rooms and Sam walked over to watch. On his way he passed the other pilots. They nodded greetings, that was all. Sam noticed that their jivebox had a vidscreen on top. As the group played on the screen a colorbar along one side gave the beat and the words streamed across the bottom. Having lived with music all his life, it looked like a pale imitation to Sam. He wondered if he would ever come to watch it, and if he did, whether he would ever enjoy it without thinking of the way things had been when he could still hear the music.

The real band finished warming up and started their set. They played old ballads, soft and sweet. It really got to Sam as he stood at the edge of the crowd. A song written by a man dead now over a hundred years was as alive as yesterday, and it made him leave the room with tears in his eyes. He stumbled out to the balcony and the music mingled with the surf. But tonight the music was stronger than the waves could ever be and it tugged at him like music had never done before.

He walked slowly out on the pier. With each step the music was fainter to his ears and stronger in his head. When he reached the end he wasn't even sure if the band was still playing. He thought he could still hear the guitar, but it was probably all in his head. He sat down on the rough wood and dangled his feet over the edge of the pier. Ten meters below him the black water lapped around the pilings in rhythmic swells as it made its way to the shore.

The sky was clear, cloudless, and the stars hung against the blackness in sharp relief. They seemed familiar now, like old friends. His training was nearly complete. He could pick out each of the visible satellites and knew their orbits by heart.

A hand touched him on the shoulder. He turned and saw it was the guitar player from the band. She handed him another Moonstar.

"Thanks," he said. "But I didn't need another one."

"We don't need a lot of things," she said. "but some of them are nice to have."

She sat quietly beside him in the darkness. He felt no need to talk and she didn't press him. The pier was damp, the stars burned brightly in the moonless sky. They would be his home soon, he felt he could almost reach out and touch them. Her hair was light blond and the ocean breeze blew it across her face.

He thought of space travel. It seemed so long ago that the dream had been born. The years had been filled with telescopes and textbooks, crowded classrooms and examinations. Like all dreams worth dreaming, it carried a high price tag. He listened to the murmur of the ocean and the music drifting from shore and weighed the price for the thousandth time.

Deafness would cut him off from people, from the casual conversations and interactions that formed the fabric of life. The circle of individuals he would be able to communicate with would shrink drastically. Then there was music, the rich soul of man. The sounds of birds, a baby's cry, a lover's moans.

But then he looked up at the stars and something else swelled deep within him. Few people had the ability to pilot the fragile ships through the twisted currents of space. It was an honor to be chosen, a privilege granted to only a handful of people. But there was more to it than that, much more.

Out among the stars, in the frozen reaches of emptiness where few could go, his soul would sing. That much he knew. In closing a door to one part of his life he would be opening another much larger door. Though he wouldn't be able to hear it, his life would be music, a dream-song to be played from his soul out there among the stars.

The woman reached out and touched Sam's arm.

"I'm cold," she said. "Let's go. I have a fireplace in my apartment."

The wind had picked up, a chill had settled in. "I don't know your name," Sam said.

"And I don't know yours."

They walked back to her apartment, a small unit on one wing of the old Coast Guard complex. It seemed to Sam that the night was full of sounds. He wanted to hold them all, freeze them in his mind. The fire crackled, the ocean churned outside the window, crickets chirped, the wind blew against the shutters. Then there were the sounds of love; flesh against flesh, the creaking of the old brass bed, the small noises they made, the whispers, the soft laughter shared. Later the sound of water in the shower. Afterwards they sat on the bed and she sang soft songs while he fell asleep.

When he awoke she was gone, a rose on her pillow, the smell of her powder in the air. The fire had gone out and the ashes were cold. He dressed quickly.

Sam drove the electric back up the coast in the fog. Once he reached the Cape he caught the first tube to the training center. Last minute tests were run, his head was shaved. He spent a restless night thinking about all the things he had promised himself he wouldn't think about.

Then they came to get him. The medication relaxed him. He was completely in their hands—there were no more decisions for him to make.

As they wheeled him into the operating room, he started drifting away. He closed his eyes to the bright lights. The last thing he remembered was the nameless girl on the bed and the beautiful songs she sang.

The Church of the One True Way wasn't the only lobby group that had come to Frost to protest the terraforming operation. There were others, chief among them a loose coalition of individuals and groups that felt the fluffers were sentient creatures, maybe even quite intelligent. At the very least, they considered them animals worthy of protection from what seemed certain annihilation.

They were a diverse group of people, ranging from wealthy ecofreaks out on a lark to highly organized committees. Unity made things as hard as possible for them, but they were required to provide space and minimal cooperation to all registered lobbyists.

Among that group was Dr. Eric Holmes, a man who brought quite a reputation with him to Frost. A short man, thin, with longish brown hair and intense deep-blue eyes, he was one of the few independent investigators who had actually set foot on the planet. What he'd seen had impressed him. More than that, it had convinced him the fluffers were sentient.

Unity Alliance, naturally enough, had been most reluctant to help him in any way. Red tape was their most effective weapon, and they used it with a vengeance. A mountain of forms fell on Eric, each to be filled out in triplicate, sworn to before a dozen officials, witnessed by as many more. Stamps and seals had to be obtained and affixed, elusive bureaucrats tracked down for additional signatures and documents—and these were just the preliminary stages. It got worse. He gritted his teeth and dug in, no stranger to the smokescreen the corporation was throwing in front of him. He'd been through it all before, several times. He'd been directly responsible for the preservation of a half-dozen alien creatures, most notably the rock dwellers of Agate.

Agate was a barren world rich in many esoteric minerals. Its discovery attracted several mining companies, who immediately divided up the planet among themselves. They then proceeded to strip it bare. Immense fortunes hung in the balance, and the balance was shifted by the discovery of the rock dwellers, the only animals on the planet more advanced than insects.

The rock dwellers were hard-shelled creatures about a meter long, looking something like a cross between an armadillo and a turtle. They lived deep in the cracks and fissures of the planet's rocky surface, in total darkness, digging complex mazes of passageways and burrows. They communicated with each other in a complicated language of grunts and clicks. This, by definition, gave them certain rights, including the right not to be exterminated.

Discovery of the rock dwellers was, of course, unreported by the mining concerns, whose operations constantly crashed through their burrows, destroying artifacts and animals alike. Quite some time passed before word of the creatures leaked out.

Eric Holmes was sent out with an investigating team to Agate in order to confirm the sentience of the rock dwellers. It turned out they had roughly the intelligence and communication ability of Earth dolphins—which is to say, considerable. Man had routinely been communicating with the sea mammals that shared his home planet for quite some time now.

The miners balked at this disclosure, tried to stall. In the end they were forced to back off. Disturbing sentient creatures on new planets was simply not done, not if anyone was watching, anyway. Laws and regulations forbid such actions, though the mechanism of enforcing these laws was spotty at best. No central government as yet bound together the many planets mankind had settled, and treaties and alliances constantly shifted. Areas of responsibility and law-enforcement authority were fuzzy and vague, often open to question.

Yet the killing of intelligent life was expressly forbidden everywhere. That much was perfectly clear.

Eric had applied pressure, turned the screws. Eventually the miners retreated to parts of the planet that were uninhabited by the rock dwellers. A study project that would not interfere with them was set up, and for the most part they were left alone.

When the question of the fluffers arose, it was logical that Eric be sent.

It took quite a while, but he finally managed to break through the red tape and get down to the surface of Frost for some first-hand observations. He was convinced.

Fluffers had excellent manual dexterity and showed the ability to use tools. Though Eric could find no evidence that they did so naturally, they picked it up readily enough. They were adept at solving mazes and simple puzzles. In addition, a fluffer who had mastered a particular maze or puzzle could teach another fluffer the solution, though they didn't appear to use a verbal language to communicate. They seemed willing to try any experiment Eric subjected them to, though they often failed to solve the more complicated ones. But to him the most convincing thing about them was an

unscientific opinion he held, a most unsup-
portable one.

There was something in their eyes, their
faces, their attitudes that spelled intelligence
to Eric. He was positive about that. Now he
had to prove it.

That was the hard part.

Morris Twelve walked through the corridors of the orbiting station with John Ten,
trying to take in everything at once. It was
their first visit to the massive satellite that
served as the nerve center for the entire operation on Frost. They were both suitably impressed. John Ten especially liked the Earth-
normal gravity. He tended to gripe a lot about
living conditions in the barracks.

Morris Twelve didn't mind the low gravity
and cramped quarters where they were staying.
He had been prepared to undergo far more
rigorous hardships than that while in service
to the church. To begin with, the phase-shift
transfer hadn't been nearly as bad as he had
feared it would be. He'd been scared going in
and sore coming out, but everything in between had been just like a restless sleep. He'd
been weak for a few days afterward, but that
hadn't really been so bad.

Their housing was on one of the captured
asteroids that orbited Frost, a half-eaten hunk
of rock that had been used as a mining station
during the preliminary stages of the project.
Now it was mostly abandoned, providing barracks for people like himself and a few labs

for the more dangerous experiments that Unity didn't want too close.

Morris was still touched by the fact that the church had chosen him to come on such an important mission, and he approached his responsibility with his customary zeal. There were only a dozen or so Unity employees on the asteroid and he talked with them every chance he got. Unfortunately, although he was dedicated, he wasn't very articulate, so when they saw him coming, they headed the other way.

This didn't discourage Morris in the slightest. He was used to much ruder reactions from people he approached on Paragon. The miners were a hard bunch, and tended to leave theological decisions to people who cared about such things. Their biggest concern was their paychecks. Keep the money coming and they were happy. All they worried about was pulling the ore out of the ground, dumping it in the driver, and tossing it where they were told.

But here on the main station it was a different story, or at least Morris thought it was. Here was where he would be able to do his best work, among intelligent people who could really influence things. They would surely see the logic and reason behind the philosophy of the One Way. There were so many people around in the large station, he couldn't help but convert a good many of them. A person was walking toward them. Morris stopped her.

"Excuse me, Pilgrim," he said. "Are you aware of the Ten Great Works of Man? The One True Way has all the answers."

Madge looked at him like he was crazy. She pushed Morris's arm away and escaped as fast as she could.

It didn't bother Morris a bit. There were other people around. Lots of them.

Teri sat still and let the wind blow over her. It was a nice feeling; cold, but good. Before her the vast bay stretched to the horizon, the slate gray water merging with the gray sky. It was beautiful. Somewhere far beyond the horizon the bay met the ocean. She'd never seen it. Someday, given the run of the planet, she hoped she'd sail it in a boat like the pictures she'd seen.

Her back leaned against a rough granite outcropping and her feet dangled over the side of a cliff. The granite rose a hundred meters above her, the waves broke against the jagged rocks fifty meters below the narrow ledge she sat on. She loved it here, alone. It was her secret place.

Teri knew she was only an hour from her next detox, but she had driven that far back into the recesses of her mind. She savored the moment, pretended it was forever. The air stung a little, but it had a fresh tang to it, it was beautiful. It was free.

Her solitude was broken by a noise, a clattering of stones, a muffled curse. Someone was coming, someone clumsy. Lan worked his way around to her perch. He was dirty and out of breath, a most unwelcome sight.

"What are you doing here?" she asked, not

bothering to hide the anger and resentment in her voice.

"I was about to ask you the same question. Hell of a place you picked."

"I wanted to be alone," she said simply.

"And I was looking for you."

"You found me. Good for you. Mission accomplished. Now you can leave. Goodbye."

He sat down beside her gingerly, testing the ground with each step before he put any weight down. He looked uncomfortable.

Lan was Teri's age exactly, to the day. He was a little taller than she, a little heavier. They had the same high cheekbones, covered with fine hair. Looking at Lan was almost like looking in a slightly warped mirror for Teri. But somehow she mostly saw the differences, seldom the similarities.

Something about him had always seemed a little childish to Teri, but she felt that way about most of her brothers and sisters, especially her brothers.

There had been no adult males in Teri's life except for the anonymous topsiders, and this had a profound effect on her attitude toward her male siblings. All the authority figures of her childhood had been females. She often had difficulty relating to her brothers and found it next to impossible to accept criticism from them, or do something when they told her to. At times they seemed almost superfluous, a token nod toward biological necessity.

"Some of us have been talking," he said nervously, searching for words.

"So what's new? You always talk too much."

"Some of the group want to go back to the dome. A lot of people don't like the detox."

Teri turned, fixed Lan with an icy stare. "Some people don't like anything," she said. "What do *you* think?"

"I . . . uh . . . I agree with you, mostly."

"*Mostly*. Thanks a lot."

"The others are saying that the detox hurts too much and it's not getting us anywhere."

"What the hell do you mean by that?" she snapped. "It's getting us the planet. What more do they want?"

Lan drew back as if she were physically attacking him. For all he knew she might be about to. He'd always been in awe of her; a little afraid of her, too, to tell the truth.

"It's not that," he stammered. "Sure, everyone wants to be outside, but this is only temporary. We can't live this way forever— even the doctors tell us that. Sooner or later we'll have to go back. Most of the people want it sooner."

"Most of the people are idiots," said Teri.

"There was a vote," said Lan quietly.

"And?"

"They voted to break camp and go back."

"They can't do that! How many voted? Who? How?"

"Everyone wanted to leave except Brit, Senne, and me. The topsiders won't stay for just the four of us, so we'll have to go. We're leaving this afternoon."

"*Idiots!*"

"They just want to go back for a while, that's all. You can't really blame them."

"Oh, yes I can. They aren't thinking ahead, they *can't* think ahead. To them, tomorrow's the distant future, next week is inconceivably far away."

"You're not being fair, Teri. The detox does hurt, there's no denying that. You and I can stand it, but they can't. It's their decision. They say they want to go back to the dome because there are more things to do there, more people to see. The food's better—"

"*Food?* What kind of people are they, putting their stomachs in front of a chance like this?"

"It's not like that, Teri. You know it isn't. You're only seeing things from your point of view. Not everyone is as driven as you are. It's not their fault it's hard out here."

"Nobody ever said it would be easy."

"Come on. We both know—"

"And you!" She turned on him again. "How come you voted to stay?"

"I wanted whatever you wanted, Teri."

"Oh no," Teri groaned, shaking her head. "Go away. Sometimes you make me sick."

"It's just—"

"Go," she said forcibly. "I mean it. I want time to think. *Alone.*"

"But—"

"I'll be along shortly. Don't worry on my account. Just leave me alone."

After he left, Teri sat feeling the bitterness course through her body like a physical presence. Fools—most of them were simply fools. They had become too dependent on comfort and the guidance of the topsiders. Someone had to break them of that and the sooner the better. It would probably be up to her. She had done all she could this time, but there'd be other times, other people. She refused to give up.

Teri scooped a small handful of pebbles and rolled them between her fingers. They were rough and had sharp edges. They were young stones, as yet unaged and smoothed by time. They were like her people, like her. One by one she threw them over the cliff.

It was too far down to the water for her to hear them or see them hit, but in her mind they made loud splashing noises and the ripples they created spread out forever in endless circles.

Madge had finished a few hours ago and she went to look at her handiwork. Her patient was walking around the conference room, testing his arms and legs. Everything seemed to be in working order.

"Feels good," Roger said, bending over and experimentally touching his toes.

"It ought to. I use only the finest equipment and replacement parts. They're the best money can buy, beg, borrow, or steal."

"They'd better be. I'd hate to think my lungs had been supplied by the lowest bidder."

"Your lungs are fine, Clown. They're still mostly natural, even if you do tend to gum them up with your dissipated lifestyle."

"No, lecture, please," moaned Roger. "I'm not in the mood today. Got a busy schedule."

"The filter packs—"

"Madge, come on. I know all—"

"In matters medical, I'm the boss," insisted Madge firmly. "I like this job too much to risk losing it because you wandered off somewhere and forgot which membrane system you were wearing. Pay attention."

Roger shook his head wearily, sat down. She was right, of course.

"Okay, you win." He threw his hands in the air, a gesture of helplessness.

"As I was saying, your nasal filters are Type Three and should be replaced every hour. The bronchial filter pack has to be changed every six hours. I tried to go with twelve-hour ones, but the organics down there are pretty tricky. Nasty stuff they have here. Better to be on the safe side, just to be sure."

Roger felt the side of his throat, ran his fingers over the small familiar patch that covered the housing for his bronchial filter pack. Sometimes they were awkward to change in the field. He'd hoped for a twelve-hour pack, or at least an eight, but Madge knew best. The nasal filters were simple plugs, easy to change.

"I had to go with the same porous sealant we used last time," continued Madge. "That should protect your pretty skin. It's just too acidic down there to even try to mess with the salves this time. I've implanted the corneal shields, as usual, the ones with the U-V screens you like. They make your eyes look yellow. I think that's tacky and vain, but what do I know?"

Sam walked into the room, waved hello, and plopped down in a chair, swinging one leg over the arm. He'd caught up on his rest and was in fine shape. Too fine, maybe. She'd heard he was back chasing after card games and women again. That boy was bound to get into trouble sooner or later.

Roger was glad Madge had decided to use the sealant this time. It was a bother to install, but a lot less trouble in the long run than the salve, which had to be constantly reapplied. Anything that cut down on maintenance in the field was fine with him. He wanted to be able to walk on the planet as naturally as a native; maybe even more so in this case, since the chimeras were having a rough time of it. In order to get the feel for the environment that he sought, he had to merge with it as closely as possible.

"It's going to be cold, so I've made some adjustments." Madge, since Sam's arrival, had started unconsciously signing as she spoke and had moved a little to one side so that the pilot could read her lips. Being around Sam was such a common occurrence to them that adjusting to it was automatic. "I've boosted your basal metabolism up quite a bit. Be sure you get plenty to eat."

"Yes, Mother," said Roger with an exaggerated sigh. "And I'll dress warmly, keep my feet dry."

"Do they have chicken soup down there?" signed Sam, grinning. Madge ignored both of them. She was used to their kidding around.

"I figure you have about seven days, maybe eight on the outside with this setup. If you want any more time than that, you'll have to come back up and let me have another shot at you. And watch your damn Bodyguard this time." Madge remembered Reality.

Reality had almost been a disaster.

The Bodyguard was a sophisticated monitoring system Madge had implanted next to Roger's spleen. It was supposed to keep close tabs on the current state of his physical condition and it did a damn fine job of it. Besides being the control center for his heart and respiration pacemakers, it watched over and evaluated a dozen metabolic factors. It was connected to a series of skin patches on the inside of his left elbow which would change color if his metabolism shifted too far in any direction. If anything went seriously wrong the appropriate patch of skin would flare red and start to itch like crazy. That would also start up a secondary alarm. Certain blood vessels would begin to constrict and produce an unmistakable ringing in his ear. This warning was almost impossible to ignore, since Madge had purposely chosen a frequency extremely annoying to Roger.

On Reality, a harsh planet full of contrasts and compromises, Roger had been deeply involved with a complex problem and, though he heard the alarm, he chose to ignore it. He solved the problem, but nearly burned out his antibody system fighting an alien virus he wasn't equipped to handle. Madge wouldn't let him forget it. That had been close—he had almost died. She'd been mad at him for that. It was almost as if she felt he had risked

damaging equipment that had somehow belonged to her. Madge was protective.

"I'll watch myself," he said, rising. "This is
only a preliminary trip, anyway. I shouldn't
be down more than a couple of days." He
started picking up some of the computer flimsies scattered around the room.

"I'll be leaving at 2200. Look around for me
while I'm gone," he said, making a neat stack
of the flimsies. "See if you can pick up anything useful. Keep your ears open."

"I'll be sure and do that," signed Sam, tug-
ging at his earlobe.

Madge groaned. *Men.* But she smiled a little,
too.

CHAPTER SIX

The glacier spread out below Roger like a river frozen in time. It sprawled across the rocks, snaked its way through the valleys between the towering peaks. The massive flow seemed to go on forever; its beginning lost in the snow and ice on the mountain range, its end obscured in a spray of jumbled cliffs at the ocean's edge. Henry Sokol set the small floater down in a level spot on the glacier and Roger got out.

The wind whipped at him, cold and sharp. He looked over his shoulder at Sokol sitting in the floater, impassive in his protective gear. Roger turned his collar up and felt the wind blow his hair. He started walking, slowly, aimlessly, letting his mind wander. The planet had a good feel to it.

The ice below Roger's feet was frosted white,

with indistinct streaks of green and blue beneath the surface. Old snow, wind-driven from the mountains on either side of the ribbon of ice, blew around him, stinging his cheeks, settling briefly on his eyelashes before melting. It felt good and he smiled. If he'd been alone he would have yelled, just for the pure joy of having his voice bounce back to him.

There was something about walking around on a planet for the first time that always excited Roger, made him feel like a kid again. Everything looked new, different. Even mundane features stood out with a sharpness and clarity as yet undulled by familiarity or repetition. These first impressions were important ones—he knew that from experience—and he saved them, mentally cataloged them, studied them. On a purely subjective level, highly unscientific and unprofessional, he also enjoyed them, savored them. There was a touch of the boy and a gram of the poet in Roger, though he would deny the existence of either one.

Frost wasn't turning out to be anything like he'd expected it to be. In spite of the material they'd sent him in advance, he'd formed kind of a mental picture of a planet nearly frozen, bitter cold from pole to pole. The more he saw of the planet, the more he realized it wasn't that way at all. Maybe it had been that way once, but things were changing.

Perhaps nowhere on the planet was the change more apparent than in the huge ocean that girdled the planet's equator. Sokol had flown him over large portions of it and he'd been very impressed. The plankton rafts, stretching in places from horizon to horizon, bobbed gently with the waves, looking like a green matted sea.

He'd visited the heat sinks, towering monolithic structures protruding from the ocean's surface, each one spreading out like a metallic octopus beneath the water. The complex formations received and dissipated the heat from Frost's distant sun, heat in the forms of energy collected and concentrated by the system of huge parabolic mirrors in orbit, beamed down to warm the ocean, raise the temperature of the planet.

Close to twenty percent of Frost remained locked in ice and snow. The glacier he was walking across was only one of many. They stretched from the poles like icy fingers, at times a hundred meters thick, kilometers wide. Many were retreating now that the planet was warming, leaving in their wake the crumbled remains of the land that had once stood in their way.

It was a lifeless area, but held a kind of crystal beauty that Roger found attractive. There was a stillness here, a feeling of solitude that man could never penetrate.

Considerable portions of the inland area of Frost were similarly lifeless, though for a much different reason. Volcanic ash and hardened lava flows covered thousands of square kilometers with a pallid grayness that bore mute testimony to the violent upheavals that had accompanied the massive alteration of the planet.

Scattered throughout these desolate places some volcanic activity still continued, huge cone-shaped mountains ripping toward the heavens, spewing ash and superheated air into the atmosphere. Steam rose from thousands of heated lakes and bubbling mud holes. Eventually the planet would reclaim this land, make it fertile again.

Roger wondered how long this restoration process would actually take. It seemed to be progressing at a phenomenal rate. Almost everywhere he went he saw interlocking networks of the rapid-growing trees. They even crept up close to the active volcano regions, advancing during lulls, being beaten back during periods of eruptions.

The terraforming scientists, of course, kept a close watch on the progress of the trees, as they were the most unusual and troublesome of Frost's surviving vegetation. In places where they wanted the land they fought the towering plants back with great difficulty. In other places they simply let them go, while continuing to watch, measure, and study them.

A large part of the planet was comprised of rough tundra, hostile, forbidding areas covered by a dense growth of small stunted plants that were apparently closely related to the trees of the more temperate latitudes. These tundra expanses, which surrounded the polar areas in both hemispheres, were subjected to periods of intense cold and seemingly never-ending winds. As far as anyone could tell, that was also as far north as the fluffers ever went.

Reflecting on that, Roger couldn't blame them. Even now, in what passed for spring, it was bitter cold. He shivered in spite of his heavy clothing, his altered metabolism.

Roger had asked Sokol to set the floater down in the tundra several times. He wandered around taking notes, gathering impressions, just getting a feel for that part of Frost.

The thick, interlocking vegetation had made walking difficult as it pulled at Roger's ankles, tugged at his feet. He forced himself to keep going, stopping often to inspect the undergrowth, collect samples of the soil. Occasionally he came across a fluffer who would eye him casually, showing no interest, no aggression, no fear.

So far Roger hadn't formed an opinion as to whether or not the fluffers were intelligent. It really wasn't his responsibility to find out, but it did have a direct bearing on how long he would be on the planet. If they did turn out to be intelligent, all bets were off and the terraforming operation would be halted. His job would be immaterial at that point and he'd head for home, paid but unsatisfied. Once he started a job, he liked to finish it.

His mind someplace else, Roger tripped on an uneven patch of ice and slipped to his knees. Startled, he brushed himself off, stood, and looked around. Henry Sokol was a speck in the distance, an impatient speck, judging by the way he was pacing back and forth by the floater. Roger had walked farther than he'd planned. He didn't remember going so far. It happened that way sometimes.

He started back toward Sokol, distracted by the towering ridges of ice on both sides of him. They looked like giant mountains of ice. The pressures that had formed them must have been tremendous. Frost was many things: unpredictable and diversified, strong.

Madge checked her instrument packs for the tenth time. They were always the same. No one else ever touched them—they wouldn't dare. Still, she checked and doublechecked them and then she checked them again. The STERILE tags on the outside of the clear packages glowed reassuringly.

Sam walked in without knocking. She gave him a half-hearted frown and he shrugged it off. If her door was unlocked he was free to come in. The years had worked that much out, and more. He looked relaxed.

"Ready to play?" he sighed.

"Play?" She shook her head, confused. She was still counting suture packs.

"You know, kick up your heels, live a little. After all, the boss is gone, leaving us this whole station to rattle around in. It's play time."

"I don't think so, Sam. I have lots to do." There were thirty-seven suture packs.

"You *always* have too much to do. You ought to get out more. There're lots of people here and lots of things to do. Let me take you dancing."

"You know there's no place here to— Oh,

Sam," she laughed, his little joke dawning on her. "You couldn't hear the music even if there was a place to go dancing."

"I don't have to hear the music," he signed, twisting his body in a fair approximation of the latest dance step. "It's all in my head." He snapped his fingers to a beat only he could hear.

"You're crazy, Sam." The years they'd shared together gave their conversation a warm glow. Old friends.

"So I've got crazy in my head. So what's new? It could be worse."

"I don't see how."

"I could be a boring person and sit around all day counting retractors." He mimed it perfectly: his face went slack and for an instant he became a dull old man, methodically counting invisible retractors hanging in empty space. She laughed.

"I wasn't counting retractors." She had seventy-two of them. Fifty-three were micros.

"I know that."

"And I'm not boring."

"I know that, too. Let's go someplace and do something exciting."

She stepped backwards and raised a suspicious eyebrow. "Like what?"

"Like dancing." His face was a mask of pure innocence: a little boy, a friend.

"I think you're serious."

"Why not? What have we got to lose?"

"Not much," she signed, looking around the room at her equipment, neatly laid out.

As they walked out the door she noted that

the defibrillator was on full charge. She stroked it reassuringly as they passed.

Roger took the lift to the basement of the dome with Henry Sokol by his side like an irritating shadow. It seemed like he hadn't been out of the man's sight since he arrived. Right now he was rambling on about the inner workings of their high-efficiency solar collectors. Roger tuned him out with equally high efficiency.

It probably wasn't Sokol's fault—almost anyone would have gotten on Roger's nerves by now. He was impatient, anxious to get things moving. At least he was about to meet some of the chimeras, the bioformed people.

The areas actually occupied by Unity and the chimeras were physically small and few in number. For the most part they were located, as was the major dome complex, on the coastal areas of the northern hemisphere. The climate was more temperate there, the winters a little warmer. That in itself was an advantage. On the other hand, the trees grew vigorously there and were more of a problem than in the more northern latitudes. It was a trade-off.

The compact city the chimeras called home was actually an extensively elaborate structure, practically two worlds under the same roof. The smaller buildings that adjoined the chimeras' dome were designed to house the administrators of the project. The atmosphere inside was such that they could work without the inconvenient life-support systems necessary everyplace else on the planet.

Calling the primary building a dome was a matter of custom rather than fact. The above-ground, rounded portion was only a small part of the structure. This was the original housing area, the place where the early generations of chimeras had lived and died in order to produce the lines that led to Teri and her brothers and sisters. When that generation appeared, a large underground system, previously unused, was opened and activated. It was three times as large as the primary area and provided housing and learning quarters for the 3,000 new residents of Frost.

As the door of the lift slid open, Roger followed Henry Sokol through an underground maze of twisted tunnels and odd-shaped rooms. He was struck by the temporary feel to everything. He felt he could easily put a fist through almost any wall, break a door by pulling hard on it. Basically it had been designed to be used once and only once—to raise the present generation to adulthood—and it showed. Roger wondered if it had been purposely built that way to give the people a feeling of impermanence, of rootlessness, to increase their desire to find a new, permanent home.

Sokol opened a door and Roger found himself inside a fairly large room filled with strangers. Most of them were chimeras, the people whose world he was trying to save. They looked him over expectantly. It was a tall order. He ignored the chair at the front of the room and instead sat among them. Introducing himself, he started to outline the basic things he was planning to do.

Teri thought Roger looked funny. To begin with he was as skinny as a stick and his pale, almost hairless skin made him look anemic and wasted. His ears stuck out like little fans and there was something strange about his eyes. She had seen Roger arrive on the planet and caught a few glimpses of him as he walked around their home. He was the first human Teri had ever seen who hadn't been totally enclosed in one of those anonymous suits.

Sitting across the table from him, he looked even funnier. It was all she could do to keep from laughing out loud.

She wouldn't dare do that. Mother Lei would kill her, and Sokol would probably skin her alive. With a great deal of effort she held her tongue and choked back her giggles while he talked.

She scarcely listened to what he was saying. Was this the man who was supposed to turn things around for them, and within her lifetime? It hardly seemed possible. Despite his obvious self-assurance he looked frail, weak in comparison to her brothers and sisters. How could this one man challenge an entire planet? How could he succeed where so many topsiders had tried and failed?

At least he was sincere, obviously concerned about her people and her planet. That was more than she could say for any of the topsiders she knew, who seemed to be interested only in complicated profit-and-loss statements of which she and her people were only one small part. The man was supposed to be good at what he did. Maybe there was a chance the stranger could do something. She'd been asked to help him. It was worth giving it all she had.

Besides, he had a nice smile. She sat back to hear what he had to say.

All this was distracting to Roger. He was trying to explain to these people what it was he wanted, but he kept tripping over his own words. The girl who had been assigned to work with him looked like she was trying hard not to laugh. For some reason that bothered him. What was so funny, anyway?

After the initial overview of the planet, Roger was ready for some close-focus, detailed work. For that he wanted to be assisted by one of the people who would be living on Frost. It would help to be able to see things through their eyes. But look what they'd given him; a woman who didn't talk much at all and seemed to find something humorous about the situation.

Roger saw nothing funny about Teri's appearance, only her attitude. He'd seen and worked with much stranger bioforms, some of them considerably less humanoid. He'd had no trouble adjusting to them. In fact, he'd enjoyed that part of the projects most of all. As heavily bioengineered as Roger was, what he felt toward the chimeras was more of a kinship than anything else.

Still, Sokol had insisted that Teri was the best assistant he could have. She knew the planet as well as anyone, maybe better. She was supposed to be intelligent and articulate, though you couldn't prove it by Roger. He had a hard time getting past her stifled laughter. But he'd take it on faith that she was a good worker. After all, she had a vested interest in having him succeed—perhaps more than she realized.

If he failed, she'd die.

Dr. Eric Holmes was finishing his cup of coffee when he saw a Truly crossing the cafeteria. He tried to slink down in his chair. They were notoriously zealous and the last thing he wanted was to have one of them babble in his ear. Morris Twelve seemed to sense this and sat down across from him.

"Hello, pilgrim," he said, smiling broadly. "Have we met before?"

The scientist sighed, set down his cup. "No," he said. "I don't believe so."

"I'm Morris Twelve of the One True Way."

"Dr. Holmes," muttered Eric.

Morris looked hard into his face. The name was familiar. It came to him.

"I know you," he said. "You work with those animals."

"I study the fluffers, yes."

"Animals," said Morris. "Animals."

"They may be intelligent," said Eric. "I think they are."

"They can't be intelligent. Only Man is

intelligent. They may be clever animals, but they have no souls, no spirits."

Eric sighed. How did he get into this? There was no reasoning with a true believer.

"I can't speak for their souls, but what I've seen of them looks very much like they are reasoning creatures."

"So is an ape, pilgrim. So is an ape."

"You can talk to an ape. An ape can reason."

Communication had been established with apes before it had with dolphins. There existed whole colonies of apes who taught each other simple sign language. You *could* talk to them, but they seldom had much to say. Mostly they liked to talk about food and grooming.

"An ape has no soul."

"You can talk to a dolphin."

"A dolphin has no soul. Only a man has a soul. Only a man can do man-things."

"I've heard this before. I'm not sure I'm convinced about this soul business."

"You don't have to believe in your soul to have one," said Morris. "Man is unique."

Morris sipped his coffee, chewed on a roll. "I wish you luck, pilgrim."

"How's that?" he asked.

"It seems to me we have the same goals. We both want this terrible thing stopped, though for different reasons. One of us may yet succeed."

"I have nothing against the chimeras," Eric said. "They are people, too. It's only that—"

"Chimeras!" spat Morris. "Lower than animals. Lower than your fluffers. They're a sin against nature."

"They're people," said Eric. "Not much different from you or me."

Morris dropped his roll to the table top. He slapped his head and chest: *I man.* "You cannot believe that."

"I believe it and it makes me sad. They have as much right to live as the fluffers, though in something like this the natural species must prevail."

"That's just choosing one animal over another."

"I don't see it that way."

"If they believe you, it doesn't matter," said Morris. "Stopping the chimeras is the only important thing. We should work together."

"I don't think so."

"Why not?" he said. "We both want the same thing."

Eric shook his head and stood up.

"I don't think we want the same thing at all," he said, turning sharply and leaving the table.

He nearly bumped into another Walker of the One True Way as he left the cafeteria. The woman smiled at him, an insipid smile, with less behind it than any fluffer he'd ever seen.

If this is man, he thought, then lord help us all.

Roger waited for Teri in the hall outside the clinic, looking for patterns on the tile floor. He was feeling better now that things had finally started moving. Once he got out into the field he became more relaxed even though he was working harder.

After a few minutes Teri came out, still a little shaky, but anxious to get the day started. They had given her the full detox treatment, good for eight or ten hours.

Yesterday had been their third time out together and she had shown him the planted fields. Teri felt good at being able to go outside, doubly good because she could stay so long. She loved it.

She greeted Roger with a broad smile. "Where're we headed today?" she asked.

"I thought I'd leave it to you," said Roger. "Where would you like to go?"

She thought a minute, biting her lower lip in concentration. "I've got an idea," she said, smiling. "Let's go someplace special."

"Sounds fine."

"It's kind of far away."

"That doesn't matter. Lead the way."

Sokol had shown Roger how to maneuver the small floater and had checked him out on it. There wasn't really much to it: up and down, left and right, fast and slow, all in one simple control stick. Although he didn't like to go very fast or high in it, he could still cover a lot of ground in a short period of time. It helped a lot.

It also freed him of the necessity of having one of the topsiders along with him. They meant well, but their presence at this stage was distracting. They had lots of facts about

Frost but, unlike Teri, very little feel for the planet. Facts he could get anytime, whenever he needed them. A feel for the planet was another thing entirely.

They walked across the paved field to the floater and climbed aboard. Teri strapped herself in without hesitation, having quickly adapted to ways considerably different than she was used to. She was really a remarkable woman, thought Roger; not at all the silly girl she had seemed at first.

Teri indicated a northwestward direction and Roger lifted the floater on its silent column of air until they were safely above the tallest trees. He eased the throttle forward carefully and they picked up speed, heading toward the distant mountains.

As the ground moved under them Teri felt no fear of the heights, only a rising joy as the land—her land—unfolded. From the air she got an entirely different perspective of the planet on which she lived. Great distances shrank, tall trees became small. She could barely make out the white specks that were the topsiders; her own people blended in too well to see clearly. The many rivers, which on the ground were only obstacles to be crossed, became twisted ribbons of silver fabric, highways of water coming from someplace, going someplace else. From the air they had purpose, direction. The wind rushing through her fur made her tremble with exhilaration.

She looked at the man sitting beside her. He seemed so serious, staring down, concentrating on the controls. She knew that either one of them could easily handle the floater, but he seemed to concentrate on everything he did. Somehow he didn't seem quite as silly-looking as he had at first. Maybe she was getting used to him, getting to know him. He *was* pretty smart, that much was obvious. Maybe he *could* do it, funny ears and all.

She grinned and started singing, a happy song full of nonsense that fit the way she felt. The wind carried it away. She waved at the people below, yelled at them even though she knew they couldn't hear her. She wanted to shout at the whole damn planet.

Roger shook his head, a smile forming on his downturned face. Sometimes she *was* a silly girl. He lifted the floater over the gradually rising foothills.

The place Teri led them to was almost four hundred kilometers from the dome, in a valley between two massive mountain ranges at the edge of one of the volcanic areas. Roger looked for a level place to set the floater down and maneuvered them into a clearing of scrubby vegetation, all dead, near a small pulsating geyser. Teri was unstrapped and bounding away before Roger had shut the engine down.

"Isn't it beautiful?" she asked over her shoulder.

"Uh . . . sure," said Roger as he looked around. There was nothing green visible for kilometers; everything was lifeless, gray, and matted. All around him steam rose from fissures in the ground, mud babbled in super-heated pools. The thick smell of sulfur hung in the air. Beautiful?

"The topsiders had a base not far from here," said Teri. "I came out here with them once. It was going to be some sort of thermal energy center, but they abandoned it. Isn't it nice?"

"It's different."

She stopped, looked at him carefully for a minute. "You don't see it, do you?"

He shook his head. "It looks pretty desolate."

"You see what you want to see. I see change."

"Change?"

She reached down and scooped up a hand-ful of the light, sandy soil, ran it through her fingers. It drifted away in the breeze.

"This land hasn't always been this way. Once it was nothing but ice and rock. The volcanos came later, after the topsiders started working, and even now they're dying out. Soon this will all be green and fertile. It changes, shifts. It grows." She kicked the dirt with her feet, stared off through the haze and mist to the mountains.

"What this place means to me is hope. It shows me that things *are* changing, that they can be different. Soon the scrub will win the fight here, then the trees will come. They'll lose battles, sure, but they'll win the war in the long run. Is it too much to hope that things will change for me, too?"

No, thought Roger. That wasn't too much to hope for at all.

CHAPTER SEVEN

Mother Lei had been watching Roger and Teri come and go for the last two days with mixed feelings. They seemed busy and seemed to be enjoying themselves. She wasn't quite sure what to make of that.

"Where are they off to this time?" asked Mother Tris. "More running around?"

Mother Tris resembled Mother Lei, but only superficially, as someone might look vaguely like a distant cousin. She was a little stockier and lighter colored. Her eyes were blue from some hidden gene and the bones in her face were subtly different, giving her a more rounded appearance.

"Waste of time," she added, looking at the two of them walking down the path to the farm. They seemed small and alone from where she and Lei sat in the observation lounge at the top of the dome. It was comfortable there, familiar. She couldn't understand why anyone would want to leave.

Mother Lei nodded. A waste of time? Maybe. It was possible, probable. "That could be true," she said.

"You know it's true," said Mother Tris with considerable feeling. "Frost's Frost. It ain't never going to be any different."

Mother Tris tended to lapse into informal gutter speech when she thought no one was paying attention. Generally it was forbidden in an attempt to keep language somewhat understandable between planetary cultures. Lei ignored it, having long ago given up trying to correct any of her sisters, especially the stubborn Tris.

"That wild Teri is one of your brood, isn't she?" asked Tris.

"Yes." Mine, my pain, my curse.

"Got three of my own around somewhere. Don't never see them, though. Of course they ain't as bright as that Teri. But they don't cause as much trouble, neither. Lose track of them, I do."

Lei nodded, her face a bleak mask as she watched Roger and Teri disappear from view. What they are doing seemed hopeless.

In spite of her deep caring for her blood-daughter, Lei almost hoped that this last-minute attempt to turn Frost around would fail. If they succeeded, Teri would be gone forever. If they failed, her daughter would have to remain in the dome, at *home*. Lei, who had watched her own mother die at an early age, did not want to be alone when her last hours came.

She thought of her mother and her mother's sisters. They had guided her and shaped her, much more than she herself had been allowed to do with Teri. The topsiders had seen to that. They had taught her games, told her stories, given her a love for life, a life bounded by walls and covered with glass. Still, it was life, a special life, a way of living that kept them going. It was a culture that would die if Frost was colonized. She couldn't bear that. And at the same time she loved her daughter. It seemed like she was always caught in the middle.

"Stupid to think they can do anything," said Tris. "It ain't natural to mess with things you can't change. Poison out there, always has been and always will be. Never any different. Ain't so bad in here, anyway, is it?"

Lei stared at a distant figure moving through the trees. She wondered if it could be her daughter.

"Is it?" repeated Tris.

"What?" She'd been daydreaming, not listening. She turned away from the large window and faced Tris. "Is it what?"

"Not so bad in here, right?"

She thought of her daughter trying to build a world out there, a world she could never live on, a world without her. The topsiders had thought of everything; everything except what really counted. The walls seemed suddenly oppressive, the glass in the window a barrier.

"I wouldn't want to be anyplace else," she lied.

The priest continued chanting in a level, monotone voice. Years of habit brought the routine phrases to his lips without conscious thought. He was bored.

It was hard for him to realize that he had once come to the church seeking solace and salvation just like those now kneeling in front of him. Hard to believe, but true. A childhood of begging and stealing in the slums of Paragon had left him drained. What he eventually found was not solace, but security. The religion didn't hold him, but the money and the power did. Like the streets, the church had a life of its own beneath the surface. It didn't take him long to realize that. Clandestine deals and graft were nothing new to him. He fit right in.

By the time he was fourteen he had things pretty well sorted out. Not everyone connected with the church was corrupt, but the percentage was high. It was enough. Before he turned twenty he had moved to the inner circle. Things moved quickly from then on. He was the youngest priest ever ordained on the planet.

The ten church members who had come to Frost with him knelt in the small room along with a half dozen converts, muttering the tired words along with him. He thought of his comfortable office back in Paragon and silently cursed the powers that had sent him to this godforsaken backwater. There was one small consolation, though. If all went well he might not have to endure this much longer.

They rose in unison at the end of the service and made the sign of man. Purified for another day, they started to file quietly out the door. There was seldom any idle chatter following the services.

This time, however, one held back. It was Morris Twelve and he looked worried. The priest sighed. More problems. It seemed they never stopped.

"You are troubled, pilgrim?" he asked after the others had left.

"Yes, priest. I carry a burden."

"We all carry burdens," said the priest, slipping into his role. "It is part of the nature of man and therefore unavoidable. Yet it is also in the nature of man to share his brother's burden, to lighten the load of his fellow travelers-in-life. Let me help you." He paused, his eyes fixed on Morris. "Is this in the nature of a confession?"

Morris Twelve looked shocked. "No," he said quickly. "Nothing like that."

"Then talk, and ease your mind." The priest flipped his hood back, consciously assuming an informal posture.

Morris fidgeted with his hands, shuffled his feet. "I'm not getting anywhere," he said. "It bothers me a lot. I don't think we're making any progress."

"We have meetings every day," said the priest. "I talk to people and I listen to them, much as you do. You report to me and I send reports back to the Vicar. Things are being done."

"I know that. You work hard. It's just that we don't seem to be getting anywhere."

"I see a larger picture than you do," said the priest. "The information we provide the Vicar about the atrocities we witness may sway planetary opinion elsewhere. Pressure can be applied to Unity, and if the pressure is strong enough, they will be forced to abandon the project."

"But *here* I can't see much happening. It's discouraging."

"You're working hard, pilgrim, doing the best you can. The church knows and appreciates this. In many ways you are too hard on yourself. You recruited one of the new members to our fold, right?"

Morris made a helpless gesture with his hands. "One man, he said in a dejected tone. "Only one man out of so many people here."

"That is one more worker for the church than there was before. Don't take that lightly, it's all important. These things are difficult, if not impossible, to measure. What is he like?"

"He was a sinner, priest," said Morris. "I found him drunk in the pits, having his way with easy women. His actions were disgusting,

a crime against the spirit of man. I believe he
has seen the light."

"Very good," said the priest. "That is an
accomplishment you can be proud of. What is
his profession?"

"A mechanic, sir. He works on small equipment." Morris was beginning to feel better. If
a man's priest approved of his actions, things
couldn't be all bad.

"Does he work on the station full-time or is
he rotated to Frost?"

"He spends a week here and a week on the
planet's surface."

One of the faithful on Frost. Interesting. Perhaps useful.

"I'll have to get to know him better," said
the priest, walking over to Morris and putting
his arm around the man's shoulder. "And as
for you, pilgrim, remember that the church is
pleased with the job you are doing here. These
are difficult times and we are working under
trying conditions. You're holding up in a man-
ner fully befitting one of the faith. Later, when
the Vicar starts things in motion, there will
be even more for us to do. I have total faith
that you will be able to carry out your part of
it."

Morris looked up at the priest like a puppy
that had just been rewarded by its master.
There was relief and pride in his eyes.

"I'll do my best," he said, straightening up.

"I'm sure you will," said the priest, thinking of ways he could use their newest convert.

Yes, another man on the planet's surface could be useful, very useful indeed.

Dr. Holmes watched the fluffer closely. The small furry animal stared back at him with large, unblinking eyes. Eric swore there was intelligence at work in the brain behind those dark-brown eyes, that light-brown face. Proving that, however, was a different thing altogether.

He'd tried tests, some standard, some of his own design. After hundreds of fluffers and hundreds of tests he still had no answer that would hold up to close examination. They showed intelligence, that much was clear—but how much intelligence? They showed some degree of self-awareness, but again the degree was open to question. Eric himself was convinced, but he had doubts he could convince others.

Eric did most of his studies on the planet's surface in a mobile van his organization had provided. Fluffers didn't take to captivity at all, having an unfortunate tendency to die after a few days, so he worked with them in the field. That way he could test them and release them unharmed.

The fluffer sat in front of him on a special table he had constructed. There were several compartments hidden beneath the table's surface that could only be reached by lifting a hinged plate. Each plate was different and needed a special key to open it. The keys were in a pile on top of the table, all similar-looking but with different tooth patterns. Eric had never worked with this particular fluffer before.

Carefully he selected a key and opened the appropriate plate, making sure the fluffer had a clear view. They were inquisitive creatures and always watched what you did very carefully. That, coupled with their lack of fear of man, made them excellent experimental subjects.

When Eric had the plate opened, he placed a cluster of berries in the hole, replacing the lid. Then he mixed all the keys together and sat back to watch.

The fluffer remained still for a few moments and then leaned over the plate, scratching at it with his long fingers. After a moment he went to the keys.

One at a time the fluffer lifted the keys and examined them. Each time he would look carefully at Eric as if anticipating encouragement. Eric would remain as still as possible, trusting that his suit would mask any visible reaction.

Eventually the fluffer picked up the right key. It seemed to Eric that it looked at him just a little longer than the other times. Then he moved over to the plate, inserted the key and opened it, removing the berries. He then put the key back in the pile and sat down, quietly munching the fruit.

There it was. Again. Nine times out of ten a fluffer would pick the right key on the first try. If it had done the experiment before it would always select the right key. But what did it mean? Were they intelligent or merely clever? And why wouldn't they do it when anyone else was around?

Eric had tried to demonstrate this experiment several times to skeptical members of the corporation. It never worked. Usually the fluffer didn't even move toward the keys, it just sat there without doing anything. Yet with him alone, it nearly always worked.

Eric shook his head, made a note in his log book. He was stumped.

Roger stood at the edge of the planted field and watched the people going back and forth working the farm. Unaided, they could only remain outside the dome for about two hours a day, but they tried to make the most of it. In addition to technological support from Unity, Frost would need a broad agricultural base when things got started.

Some worked in the gardens, others busied themselves elsewhere. The air was filled with the hum and buzz of saws felling trees. Several cabins had been completed; others were in various stages of construction. At first the chimeras could use Unity's buildings, but it wouldn't be long before they outgrew them and would have to spread out.

He had been standing there for several minutes before he realized something felt odd, a little out of kilter. Then it dawned on him that there were no old people, no children. All the people within view were approximately the same age. It made sense, of course, but he hadn't really thought about it before. The older people, the Mothers, weren't able to leave the dome, and as yet, none of Teri's generation had children. Everyone outside had been born within a couple of years of each other. They had been raised under identical conditions. Upon reflection, Roger was surprised they weren't even more similar, both physically and emotionally.

Some were smarter than others, some larger, stronger. They differed in a thousand ways. They were individuals. The one thing they shared was a desire to leave the confines of the dome and start their lives outside. It was enough.

Lan walked by, detached himself from the small group of people he was with, and approached Roger.

"You've been around here so much we might as well give you a tiller and put you to work," he said. "We could use the help."

"I wouldn't mind it," said Roger.

"Anything happening?" asked Lan. They all asked that. Roger heard the question a hundred times a day. He couldn't blame them, they were bound to be anxious.

"Not much new," he said. "I'm still getting my Frost legs."

"Have you seen Teri?"

"Not lately." Teri was taking full advantage of her access to the intensive detox procedure. When she wasn't outside with Roger, she was usually wandering around on her own somewhere.

"If you see her, tell her I'm looking for her. Nothing important," said Lan.

"I'll do that."

Walking to the edge of the field, Roger sat down on one of the felled trees. It was huge, with thick and heavily convoluted bark. The tree seemed to have two distinctly different kinds of limbs. The upper branches were the usual type; thick with broad leaves. Lower down the branches were thin and leafless, almost like vines. The end of each of these limbs was drawn up into a tight ball of coiled tendrils. Each tree had a lot of them.

The trees were complex plants and remarkably adaptable. They grew more rapidly than they had any right to. Unity was constantly trying out different defoliants on them, but never had much success. A new compound might work for two or three days but then the trees would develop a resistance and come back even stronger.

Somehow the resistance the trees developed wasn't confined to the infected area, like it should have been. Trees all over the planet would suddenly become immune to the defoliant. It didn't make sense, but there it was: a fact. Frost was a strange planet.

Roger shifted his weight and watched a fluffer sitting in the branches of the downed tree he was resting on. The animal seemed oblivious to him and went about his business as if Roger wasn't there.

After seeing so many of them in the last few days, Roger was fairly certain that the fluffers were non-sentient creatures. He hadn't seen them doing anything that remotely suggested intelligence, which was just as well. That would stop the terraforming project and Roger didn't want that, not now. He'd come to the point where he wanted to bring around Frost as much as the chimeras did. They were good people, they deserved to live.

The fluffer was gathering berries from the tree, stuffing them in his mouth, filling the pouches in his cheeks. After a short time he hopped off the tree to the ground. Digging a series of small holes, he buried some of the fruits. Others he sat and ate. Unconcerned, he eventually wandered off.

After the animal left, Roger dug up one of the berries with a stainless steel probe and carefully placed it in a sample bag. As an afterthought he picked a fresh berry off the tree and dropped it in another bag. He'd send them up to the boys in the lab, give them something to play with. Probably nothing would come of it. He'd sent other kinds of samples up before with no startling results. It would keep them busy for a while, anyway. They claimed they could analyze any sample down to its last molecule. He'd give them a chance to prove it.

There were eighty-seven moving parts in the gear box of a floater and he knew every one of them like an old friend. The retaining spring came off easily in his hand and the two primary cogs slipped free. He started to clean them.

Drew Cooper had a way with machines. You could put him in front of nearly anything mechanical and within an hour he'd have it figured out. It was the only talent he had.

Almost everything else in Drew's life was a total disaster, or at least it had been before he saw the light and followed the path of the One True Way. He blessed Morris Twelve for saving him from a life of sin and self-destruction. Taking the name of Drew Seven, he put most of his life in the church's hands. It was a load off his mind.

Having people take control over parts of his life was nothing new to Drew. His parents had done it first, with a vengeance. Next, his teachers at the trade guild took over the task, then the various people he worked for. It wasn't all bad, though. In a way he liked it. It saved him from making decisions, and he'd never been very good at that.

Drew wasn't very bright. He left reasoning and abstract thinking to other people. Let them worry about things like that. The only time in his life he was really happy was when he was working on machines. Everything else just got in the way.

Lately even the women had been getting in his way. They and the gin had been about to kill him. All his money seemed to be dropping down a hole. He'd been in debt for his next three paychecks when Morris had fished him out of the sewer.

The church paid off his debts and dried him out. That was fine with Drew, he was most grateful. Anyone who did that for him had to be all right.

They didn't want much from him in return, either; not like the loan sharks who had gotten him out of other fixes. All he had to do was memorize the phrases and learn how to talk the church up in front of other people. That wasn't hard. He'd never liked the chimeras that much anyway. The church had been good to him, real good. He'd do whatever it wanted him to do.

He tightened a bolt, really cranking down on it. It seated itself as if it had been welded there. He had powerful hands.

Teri was laughing and sweating as she knocked Roger to the floor. In the interests of good sportsmanship, he asked her to help him up. In the interests of competition, she sat on him until her team scored the winning point. The gymnasium rang with cheers and groans. *Then* she helped him to his feet.

Roger had yet to get the hang of the game they played, a game with simple equipment and complicated rules. They pushed a ball around with sticks and tried to get it between opposing goals. There were several goals—wire hoops of various sizes—and they all scored differently. The only thing Roger had managed to figure out was that you were supposed to keep the opposing team from getting the ball through any of the goals. He wasn't any good at the game, but he tried. The important thing was that they had invited him to play.

After the game was over they sat on the floor talking and laughing, telling jokes. It was a relaxed time and Roger slid right into the warm, close feeling. They talked about anything and everything, both the special things that tied them to Frost and the ordinary concerns of ordinary people. Lan had

just returned from a short trip to Mountain-
top and everybody wanted to know what it
was like, as few of them had ever been there.

Their curiosity about Frost was endless and
they constantly probed Roger for more information. It was obvious they valued his ideas
and impressions. Some of their questions were
technical, but most were general. They wanted
to know everything.

Lan had a question about some rock formations he had seen on his trip and Roger answered as best he could. A lot was known
about the planet, but much more was unknown. In the end, they would have to find
out most of it by themselves.

When Lan finished, Mila told an off-color
joke about three topsiders trying to make love
with their suits on. It was an outrageous tale,
carried to ridiculous extremes. They all laughed,
including Roger.

Although Roger was technically working for
the topsiders, it was plain he was not considered to be anything like them. The chimeras
thought of him as their friend, their ally. He
was closer to them than the white-suited, faceless ones. Roger walked among them unencum-
bered, played with them, often worked along-
side them. He cared and it made a difference,
a considerable difference.

Things were shifting and Roger could sense
it, both in the way they felt about him and
the way he felt about them.

They had accepted him into their group and
he didn't mind at all. It had happened once or
twice before on other planets, other jobs. But

this was a little different. All the other times
he had been simply drawn into their lives as a
natural result of working closely with them.
He had been neutral about it, not really caring one way or another. Either way the job
got done.

But this was different. The more he had
gotten to know these people, the more he liked
and respected them. They were hard workers;
dedicated, friendly people who were trying to
make the best of a difficult situation.

By now the job he had come to do had become more than a job. Somehow it had gotten
all tangled up inside him. He *cared* for these
people, they were special.

He watched Teri laugh and was torn by
conflicting emotions. He wanted to laugh with
her, to share the humor and lightness of life
with her and her people. Yet deep inside him
there was a cold dark knot tied tightly by fear
and despair. If he could somehow help change
Frost, she and her people would scatter to the
winds. The planet that could support her could
not support him for very long.

If he failed, he could be with her in the
halfway situation of the dome for an undeter-
mined amount of time, until Unity quit main-
taining it or she died. Eventually the poisons in the dome would build up and kill her
in spite of the daily detox. Without her planet
she was doomed and they both knew it.

For an instant Roger felt alone to a degree
he had never experienced before, not even when
he had been the only human standing on a
distant and isolated planet. He was different

from these people in a very fundamental way. He was living a life and they were living a death sentence. Only he could change it for them.

And if he changed it he would lose them, lose them all. Forever.

The laughter snapped him out of his reverie and Lan brushed his arm in friendship, following up something he had just said that Roger had missed. It was an easy touch, casual, with no awkwardness about it. Teri stood to his left and giggled at his quizzical look.

"Dreaming again?" she asked. "Or working?"

"A little of both," he said, feeling embarrassed where he had no need to be.

He reached out and tousled her hair as he might a small child's. It was fine and smooth, silky.

He laughed outside to cover his embarrassment, but what he felt inside when he touched her was confusion, a mixture of emotions that ranged from parental concern to lust. He knew he shouldn't have any of them.

But he did.

CHAPTER EIGHT

Sam was getting restless. He often felt this way after they arrived at a new planet and he had time on his hands. It was a letdown that always seemed to follow the intense activity and concentration during transit. It usually lasted until he could find out where the local poker games were held. Also, he looked for other pilots he could talk to. Usually the two were found in the same place.

"How many trips so far?" signed Sam. He was talking with Lou, one of the pilots who ran back and forth between Frost and Paragon.

"Eight," signed Lou, a heavy-set man a little older than Sam. "It's not a bad hop. Takes about ten hours or so. Two or three tricky maneuvers, but most of it is straight ahead. A piece of cake."

"Shut up and deal," signed another pilot,

flipping the cards to Lou. He shuffled them expertly, the silver implants in his hands flashing, and dealt five-card draw.

Sam picked up his cards, a pair of kings. He didn't improve on them and lost to three sevens. He tossed in a marker to cover the ante.

While the cards were being dealt Sam looked around the crowded lounge. Several poker games were going on at different tables. Two people were playing go; another pair was involved in a strange game with small blocks of wood. In the corner a poker player was bitching in sharp, angry gestures, swearing that he was going to buzz another pilot who had crossed him.

One disadvantage that talking in sign language brought about was that it was nearly impossible to have a private conversation. If you could see it you could read it, no matter how far away.

Just as the cards landed in front of Sam, someone entered the room, ranting and raving. He was speaking, not signing, but Sam had no trouble understanding him. He was cursing them, calling them sinners to the core, exhorting them to repent before it was too late. Trulies really turned Sam off.

"Who's that?" he signed, turning back to the game.

"Cooper. A mechanic. Reformed boozer and doper. Crazy as a bug."

"Reformed dopers are the worst," signed

Sam. Then he picked up the cards and shuffled them, ignoring the silently yelling man.

He was only barely aware of the nondescript man who came with him, the one who walked around the room quietly talking to anyone who would listen, trying to use his own brand of reason and logic just as Cooper used his righteous anger.

When he walked by Sam's table he kept going. An independent bunch, pilots were nearly impossible to convert. They only heard what they wanted to hear. Sam was concentrating on his cards, trying to fill an open-ended straight, when Morris Twelve walked by. He never even looked up.

The fitting for the high-pressure bypass valve was behind the transmission housing, and a bitch to get at. After a few minutes of fussing, he managed to get a wrench on it and give it a quarter-turn. Vibration would take care of the rest.

It would hold fine until the lift pressure reached a certain level, at which point the bypass valve would be triggered. Normally it was a blow-by system and the excess pressure would be recycled back into the lift mechanism. Loosening of the valve would cause pressure to be lost at a critical point.

The floater would crash.

Roger had just returned with Teri from an excursion to the central plateau. He'd collected about twenty sample bags of miscellaneous material for the lab to look over. He was sure they hated him by now—he must have increased their workload by a factor of fifty. He tended to follow his hunches in the field. If something caught his interest he'd check it out. Most of the time nothing came of it, but you could never tell when something significant might pop up out of nowhere.

Roger had enjoyed their trip to the plateau. He loved the feeling of isolation he got in places on the planet like that. There couldn't have been another person for a hundred kilometers or more. He'd even gotten used to the sharpness of the air, the metallic aftertaste. They'd wasted time out there, just walking, talking. Teri had told him some of her dreams for the planet, the plans she had for the day when she and her siblings could live on it forever. She painted a magical, optimistic picture of a land where the people and the rest of the planet lived side by side in harmony. Maybe they would; Roger hoped so. The more he saw of Frost, the more he liked it. He'd seen a lot of it, too, with more to come. Later this afternoon he was planning on a trip to an island chain that jutted into the ocean.

"Are you sure you can't come?" he asked.

"I'd love to," said Teri, "but they messed up my schedule again. I'm headed for an hour of detox and then I've got to go put in my shift in the fields."

"You won't change your mind?" he asked. "I'm headed for the north side this afternoon.

There's supposed to be some new activity out that way."

He almost had her there. She loved that place. But she smiled at him and that was her answer: *you know me better than that; I have to help my people.*

"At least I can walk you over," he said.

"Sure."

He handed the floater's log book to the mechanic and gathered up his sample bags. Together they started across the hard-packed dirt of the landing field.

Walking side by side like that they made a most curious couple. Roger looked positively gaunt and lanky next to her, though he didn't feel either. Teri only came to his chest, but she moved with an easy, cat-like grace. He always felt awkward beside her, but it never really bothered him. Possibly that was because it never bothered her.

"What's that?" she asked as they neared the dome, pointing to his arm.

He looked down. "Nothing," he lied. "Just a rash."

It wasn't a rash and he knew it. His Bodyguard, the built-in monitoring system, was starting to protest. Roger could tell from the location and color of the small mark that it was a preliminary respiratory warning. Nothing to really worry about, not yet. It always got a little sensitive after a few days in the field. More than likely it would go away after he changed his nasal plugs. Roger knew he should have gone back up yesterday—Madge was already bitching at him—but that couldn't be helped. He was busy right now. The volcanic samples he wanted had to be taken today, at an activity peak. He didn't trust anyone else to take them. He'd go back tomorrow after they went to the islands. That should be in plenty of time. He figured Madge, like most doctors, tended to play everything on the conservative side anyway. He could set things up for a one day turnaround and come right back down.

He left Teri at the clinic, making arrangements to meet her after he got back from collecting his samples, probably late afternoon or early evening.

For some reason it seemed far in the future.

Madge was furious, boiling mad. She stormed around her room fussing with everything in sight, cursing and muttering under her breath. How could a supposedly intelligent man be so stupid, so careless? He had no right to take such foolish chances. She moved a stack of flimsies from her desk to the top of her dresser, paced around the room twice, and moved them back to her desk. She was about to put them back on the dresser when someone knocked on her door.

"Go away," she said.

The door opened and Sam walked in.

"I told you to go away," she snapped.

"Sorry," he signed. "I seem to have trouble seeing through doors these days."

She stopped short, embarrassed. "I'm sorry,

Sam," she signed. "I wasn't thinking. Too upset."

Sam sat down on the edge of her bed. "What's the problem?" he signed. "You drop someone's kidney on the floor?"

"That's not funny. Roger hasn't come back yet."

"So the boss decided to stay an extra day. What's the big deal? Maybe he wanted a vacation."

"He was supposed to come back up yesterday, you know that. When he wasn't on the shuttle I tried to get in touch with him. It took me half the night, and when I finally got him, he wouldn't listen to reason. He's got some crazy idea about coming back tomorrow instead. Says he's following up on something interesting. *Everything's* interesting to that man, Sam. He's got no sense of responsibility. Now he won't even answer my calls."

"I don't blame him," signed Sam. "You'd only nag at him."

"Sam!"

"It's true. Come on, Madge, you know that much. How many years has it been?"

"Too many."

"And you still play the game, both of you."

"What game?"

"You always tell him to come back two days early and he always comes back two days late. It's a game. He didn't *have* to be back yesterday, did he?"

"I try to be on the safe side."

"He didn't really have to be back that soon, did he?"

"It would have been better if he had."

"But he's still okay, even if he comes back tomorrow. That's the truth, isn't it?"

Madge nodded.

"I'm sure he knows that, too, just as well as you do. Roger's not going to take any real chances down there, he's too much of a professional. Besides, he's got his Bodyguard. That'll warn him of trouble in plenty of time."

"If he remembers to watch it. *If* he pays attention to it."

"You just like to worry, Madge," signed Sam. "My mother was like that, too. It used to drive me up the wall. Gave her ulcers. It never helped either one of us much."

"I don't like to take chances," she said, straightening the stack of flimsies and putting them on the dresser. "I'd rather play it safe."

Roger took off from the field and headed north. Since he was going farther than he usually did, he flew a little faster and a little higher. The dome quickly fell behind him. He left the valley through a pass in the mountains that Sokol had shown him. When he emerged on the other side, the trees were a blanket of solid green far below him. On the distant horizon he could see the mountain cascades and the thin haze of smoke that hung over the area. The distances were deceptive, though, and it took him longer to get there than he'd expected.

First Roger circled the area checking things out and getting a general feel for the land. The reports had been correct; there seemed to be a lot of new activity. On the northwest side, lava was oozing from fissures in the ground and spreading out like a thick, molten carpet. One part of the flow was moving into a forested section, toppling trees as it pushed through. The whole area sparked with scattered balls of fire as the massive plants reached kindling temperature and burst into flames.

Not far away a good-sized lava lake nestled within an irregular ring of jagged rocks. This he'd seen before. It seemed to be a permanent feature of this volcanic region. As permanent, that is, as anything was in an area that shifted so much. Fountains of lava several meters tall spurted up in the middle of the molten lake, driven by building pressures in the fissures below the ground. The lava would come crashing back to the surface of the lake and roll out toward the edges, leaving behind a glowing red trail. It was a highly active area, just what he wanted.

A small cone was slowly forming in the middle of all this activity. There was no telling what might become of that. It might explode and be blown away, or it might keep going like it was, eventually reaching a tremendous size. Or then again, it might just drop. These things were next to impossible to predict.

Roger's primary purpose was to collect gas samples in an attempt to see how much this

area—and areas like it all over the planet—
contributed to the excess acid concentration
of the atmosphere. He was also going to take
particulate counts in order to measure how
much solid material was being thrown into
the air from these constant minor eruptions.
A mechanic had strapped sampling contain-
ers to the underside of his floater so Roger
could do his collections without having to
land, though he would have to make a couple
of tricky dives near the surface. He'd practiced them with Sokol looking on and had
never had any problems. If he had time he
might set down and collect some rock samples,
but that was secondary to his main purpose.

The sample canisters were controlled by a
switching box he had strapped to the empty
passenger seat. When the floater was in the
right position, he would trigger the appropriate canister and collect his sample. The first
two were easy, high-altitude ones. For the third
one he had to drop down to about twenty
meters and skim the surface of the lava lake.

Even twenty meters above the surface and
protected by the body of the floater, Roger
could feel the intense heat of the molten lava.
He gathered his sample quickly and hit the stick
hard to put himself in a sharp climb and get
away as soon as possible.

Just as the nose of the floater started pointing upward, he heard a dull knock followed
by the hiss of gas escaping somewhere. The
controls went dead in his hands.

He fell like a rock.

*   *   *

Teri was planting seedlings. This crop seemed to be holding up much better than the previous ones. On the other hand, maybe it was simply that her attitude was improving. Things in general seemed to be going a lot better. She straightened up and rubbed her back, sore from so much bending over. Lan was chopping wood off to one side of the field. He waved and she waved back. Two more rows and she would be finished for the day. Each seedling had to be carefully planted by hand, the soil packed around it with just the right amount of pressure. It felt good to be working outside, but she was looking forward to seeing Roger tonight. It would be fun to go to the islands with him tomorrow, to see the ocean.

A cold wind blew across the field. A zephyr, it came at odd intervals down from the mountains. This one sent a shiver through her. She didn't like the feeling and bent back down to her work.

It hit her again, sending a chill up her spine.

CHAPTER NINE

Light flickered through his agony, brief flashes of crackling sparks amid the sharp, stabbing pain. With difficulty, Roger forced his eyes open and blinked the blood and sweat out of them. Everything was blurred, out of focus. Blood dripped from his chin to his nose, so he realized he was upside down. It hurt to breathe.

He fumbled with the chest release to his safety harness. Everything was twisted around and it was hard to reach. His fingers fumbled clumsily at the clasp. When it snapped free he didn't fall, as he'd expected. His legs were jammed between the seat and the control panel, holding him in place. Awkwardly he worked his way loose.

Roger crawled through the shattered canopy and collapsed beside the wreckage of the crushed floater. He coughed, and the sharp taste of blood was in his mouth. If Madge could see him now she'd have a fit. The thick sulfur smell was everywhere. He suddenly realized it was hot.

The floater was a tangled mess, one side of it completely sheared away. It was wedged upside down at the base of a towering rock formation. No one could possibly see it from the air.

Roger stood and tried to get his bearings. His legs were shaky; he had to hold onto the rocks to keep his balance. He didn't like what he saw.

He was down someplace between the molten lake and a slowly moving lava flow. The lava wasn't moving slowly enough, though. He estimated it would reach the floater in about fifteen minutes and he didn't plan to wait around for it.

There was only one real sanctuary—the forest that ringed the volcanic area. It seemed incredibly distant, but it was the only safe place. He fought back the pain and started out.

He found himself crossing a no man's land, a desolate and lifeless area. The ground was uneven and shifting, much of it covered by ash that varied in thickness from a thin coating to a blanket several meters thick. He stumbled constantly and was completely covered with gray ash. Steam rose from fissures all around him. Sweat streaked the ash on his face and turned it to mud.

The lava flow had completely swallowed what was left of the floater. It was moving about twice as fast as he could walk and had already cut off the shortest way to the forest. The flow was about four meters high and had the consistency of thick oatmeal. The cooler parts on the surface were black, but in the cracks he could see the fiery red interior as it made its steady way across the land, oozing around only the sturdiest rock formations, pushing the rest out of the way, igniting anything flammable that remained in this hellish place.

The inside of Roger's left arm was lit up as his Bodyguard protested what he was forcing himself to do. His support systems were starting to fail. He ignored it. He had to; there simply wasn't anything he could do about it, not now.

He pulled himself over a pile of hardened lava, his hands and feet throbbing with pain. In front of him lay a crystal pool of clear water at least sixty meters across. His heart sank. Through the unbroken surface he could make out the bottom distinctly. Under different conditions it would be beautiful; now it reeked of death. Ripples of heat stirred the water; it was just below the boiling point. Another detour. He moved around it, picking his way across the rocks.

Just as he left the water behind him, a finger of the lava flow reached the edge of the pool and spilled into it. A deafening explosion tore at him as a tower of steam rose in a billowing cloud, filling the sky. He could feel the moist heat baking him. He bent his head down, covered the back of his neck with his hands, and kept going.

The farther he went, the farther it seemed he had to go. He stumbled constantly. His chest was about to burst. Twice the ground shook and twisted beneath his feet as earthquakes tore at the land. He fell, picked himself up, and kept on going.

The sun was setting now, and the whole area became a surreal landscape. A dull red light colored everything, chasing the darker shadows. Blue and green flashes marked gas explosions. The air was filled with sparks and deep rumbling noises. The forest was still an impossible distance away, and the pain had passed all measure now. It was either keep moving or die. He kept moving.

Teri paced around the walkway that surrounded the observation level of the dome. It was really too early for her to expect Roger back, especially if he'd found something interesting. Teri knew by now that he was easily sidetracked. Some little thing would catch his eye and he'd spend hours looking at it, losing all track of time. She'd seen it happen before.

Below her, the next shift was heading out to work. That would be the last group out before dark. She watched them as they disappeared down the path that led to the fields, feeling a warm kinship toward her brothers and sisters. It seemed that they were really making headway these days.

Roger would return before dark. Teri was certain about that. He didn't like to work alone in the field after nightfall.

Maska came out onto the walkway and talked with her for a while. Supposedly she'd come to talk with Teri about a new fertilizer they were field-testing. Mostly she just wanted to gossip. Maska was terrible about that. Usually Teri could at least feign interest, but this time she couldn't even manage that. All the time Maska was talking, Teri scanned the sky anxiously. Even though it was early, it wouldn't hurt to keep an eye out for him. He could be back at any time. Any speck on the horizon could be a floater, and any floater could be Roger. But there weren't any specks.

When darkness came, Teri's concern turned to panic. It wasn't like Roger not to return when he'd planned to. If he were going to be delayed, he would have let her know somehow. She tried to see if anyone had heard from him and ended up talking with Henry Sokol.

"No, he hasn't checked in yet, but I wouldn't worry about it," said the topsider. "He's probably just doing some nocturnal studies. I know he had some planned."

"Not for tonight," said Teri. "I *know* he didn't. He told me he'd see me later."

"He's a busy man. Maybe something came up."

"He would have let me know. He wouldn't have forgotten. That's not like him."

"He's a grown man, Teri. He can take care of himself."

"Would you at least try to call him?"

"We already have," said Sokol.

"And?"

"And nothing. No answer."

"Can't you see? Doesn't that mean—"

"It doesn't mean anything. He could have his communicator turned off. Or he could be away from the floater. There are a thousand possible explanations."

"I'm afraid," said Teri. "I know something's happened to him, something bad."

"If he's not back by morning, we'll go looking for him. Will that satisfy you?"

"Only if I can go along."

Sokol agreed, but that didn't make Teri feel any better. The whole thing made her sick with worry. The morning was a long way off. Anything could happen.

Maybe it already had.

Maybe Sam was right, thought Madge. Sometimes she was a little overprotective. But she couldn't help feeling that way—it was part of her nature. Besides, Roger *should* take better care of himself.

Actually, it wasn't too bad yet. He'd be in good shape as long as he was on the shuttle tomorrow. Any longer than that would be pushing it too far. His tracheal pack would have to be changed. His kidneys were probably all clogged up by now. She'd have to flush his whole system out. That would take a couple of days at least. He wouldn't like it, but that was too damn bad. If he took better care of himself, he wouldn't have to go through it so often.

Madge shifted in her bunk, restless. She was having trouble getting to sleep. It was silly to worry so much, but she couldn't help it. In addition to her professional involvement with Roger, she cared deeply for him as one old friend cares for another. They had been through a lot together.

She gave up trying to sleep and got out of bed, slipping on some old clothes. It wouldn't hurt to check with the communications people and see if Roger had called in yet or left a message. It had been over two hours since she last checked with them. He could have called. He was probably having trouble with his transmitter, something simple like that. It was always something simple that caused the most trouble.

Maybe Sam was wandering around somewhere. They could sit down and have a cup of coffee or something.

Mostly she wanted somebody to talk to.

Sam closed his eyes, taking himself out of the conversation. It was rude, a breach of etiquette, but he didn't care. Drifter Pete and Carolyn were busy lying to each other about past misadventures, each trying to outboast the other. Their hands were flying and Sam just didn't feel like following along. He closed his eyes and the music came.

Through the years of silence, music had measured his moods. It comforted him in times of trouble, lifted his spirits in times of joy. Although it was simply the echo of music years gone, it lived for Sam and filled an empty spot in his life. Unlike those who had been deaf from birth, Sam had his memories to draw from. They helped.

As he drifted in the silent darkness, farther and farther away from the animated conversation of the other two pilots, it seemed to him as if a solitary guitar was far across that room, quietly weaving a tapestry of classical music at the very edge of the hearing he knew he didn't have. He flowed with it for a minute, gathering his thoughts, and was worried. Madge was right.

Roger was cutting it too close, and that wasn't like him. No matter how busy he'd gotten, he'd never lose track of the safety factor. It was too important. Even when he'd been playing those games with Madge, the margin for error had been there and he'd never seriously pushed it. This was just too damn close. Something was wrong.

Sam felt he'd done the right thing in trying to take Madge's mind off Roger. She *did* worry too much, no question about that. On the other hand, there hadn't been any word from him since then. A bad sign.

As much as they'd been together, Sam had difficulty imagining Roger in real trouble. He'd seen the man in bad situations before, but nothing he couldn't handle. Roger had a way of landing on his feet, making the best out of a lousy situation. Hell, some of the scrapes they'd found themselves in had been pretty tight, but Roger always managed to get through. Frost was a tough planet, but there had been tough planets before, and there would be tough planets again. Maybe.

What hurt was the waiting, being stuck up in orbit.

A tug on his arm pulled him away from the guitar, but not the worry. He opened his eyes.

"We're going down to the pits to find some action," signed Drifter Pete. "You want to come along?"

Sam shook his head. There ought to be something they could do. Anything would be better than this waiting. "No," he signed. "Not this time."

Carolyn laughed soundlessly. "She must be quite a woman, whoever she is. I never saw you turn down an invitation to the pits."

Sam stood up and kicked his chair back with anger and frustration. He turned away abruptly, leaving the two pilots staring at each other. He had to find Madge.

Another tremor shook the ground, this one even stronger than the ones before. The world tilted crazily beneath Roger's feet. He tried to keep his balance but failed, tumbling headfirst into a deep blanket of ash.

He struggled to his feet, spitting the gritty particles from his mouth, wiping them from his eyes. The ash was everywhere. He stumbled blindly forward, thinking of nothing but survival. Lightning flashed all around him;

from the sky, from the ground. Rolling peals of thunder were mixed with the dull thumps of nearby explosions. He lost all sense of place and time. It took everything just to keep lurching forward. If he was moving he knew he was still alive.

When he bumped into the first tree he didn't recognize it. To him it was just another obstacle to go around, another thing to be avoided. The bark scraped his face as he rolled around it, only to fall against the trunk of another one. Suddenly he realized where he was. He'd made it to the forest.

The trees were on slightly higher ground than the lower volcanic area. They sloped in a gentle rise up away from the roaring inferno. He felt like screaming for joy, but he had no voice left. Only a rasping hiss escaped his mouth when he tried. As darkness surrounded him, he fought his way through the trees seeking even higher ground.

Roger pressed on for hours, his pain lessening somewhat, replaced by a dull ache. He wanted to rest, but didn't dare stop. It was getting difficult to breathe, and he wondered how much longer his support systems would last. Their failure would probably kill him before anything on the planet could get to him. The tremors were picking up. A piercing shriek filled his ears, growing in intensity. It sent a shudder through him, and it was a moment before he could place the sound.

The noise was fluffers, fluffers in blind panic. It was a distinctive sound, high-pitched and drawn out like the death wail of some exotic monster. It drilled through Roger's head as the ground started rolling and pitching beneath him.

The trees around Roger started to creak and groan as they swayed with the shifting ground. Several fell crashing to the ground. One barely missed Roger, its branches raking the side of his body.

Fluffers were everywhere, screaming, screeching, running in blind panic. It was a nightmare. They filled the trees, covered the ground, scampered over one another in their haste. Their screams rose in pitch, and Roger felt the cold sweat of fear.

Something was about to blow. He could feel it as surely as the fluffers. He had to get out of there. Jarring himself into motion, he followed the small animals. A series of muffled explosions came from somewhere behind him. He doubled his efforts, pushing his protesting body even harder.

Time blurred. The only thing that mattered was getting past one more tree, putting that much more behind him, between him and whatever was going to happen in that place he'd just left. The fluffers screeched along with him. The first light of dawn was in the sky when it came.

He felt the explosion more than he heard it. A rocking concussion lifted him into the air, tossing him like a rag doll into the lower branches of a nearby tree.

Behind him he could see an angry boiling

cloud of gasses climbing toward the sky. All around him the trees were snapping like twigs, falling to the ground. His ears rang, and it felt like every bone in his body was broken. Lightning flashed continuously inside the rising plume, and a searing wind swept over him.

It looked like the end of the world.

Teri thought so, too. Her heart sank as she watched the terrible mushroom cloud rise into the morning sky. Nothing could have survived that, nothing. Even from the floater fifty kilometers away it looked monstrous.

"Are you sure that's where he said he was going?" asked Henry Sokol.

Teri nodded, her eyes riveted to the churning mass. As horrible as it was, she couldn't take her eyes off it.

"Maybe he went someplace else," he said. "He could have changed his plans."

"Maybe," said Teri in a flat, emotionless voice. She didn't think so.

"We can't do anything now," he said. "After things calm down we can send a search party in."

"I knew something was going to happen," said Teri. "I *knew* it."

"If he's out there, we'll find him," Sokol said.

Teri stared at the boiling cloud of death and felt nothing but despair. They would never find him. Never.

CHAPTER TEN

The nightmare never stopped. For hours the ground rattled with tremors, the sky split and cracked. The rising volcanic cloud blotted out everything, swallowing the sun and turning day into night. Roger moved constantly, determined to escape the inferno that raged behind him.

He worked his way up the side of the sloping foothills, keeping pace with the fluffers. He felt a deepening kinship with the simple animals. They shared the same fate. In delirious periods he shouted encouragements to them, urging them on. The fluffers were his comrades, his only companions.

The upward slope of the land steadily increased and at times, Roger had to pull himself up steep sections with his hands. Twice he scaled vertical cliffs when there seemed to be no easy way around.

Hanging on the side of one of these cliffs, Roger had an unobstructed view of the place he'd left behind. Devastation of the valley was nearly total. Black clouds hung over the whole area like a low canopy, hiding the distant mountain peaks. The volcanic activity showed no signs of lessening. All he could do was keep going.

Without realizing it he crested a small ridge and started downhill. The going was a little easier, but it lessened the chances of anyong finding him soon.

Then the rains started, a sharp, cold rain driven by ever-increasing winds. The ash became mud and it was everywhere. Lightning silhouetted the branching trees above him and thunder rolled constantly in his ears. He lost his footing and slid downhill for a couple of meters.

The fluffers were no longer moving along with Roger. In the flashes of lightning he could see their small bodies curled up tightly in the branches of the trees. It was becoming difficult even to stand up. He leaned against the wind and pushed on.

Roger's Bodyguard was sending him frantic warnings that he was forced to ignore. The rain was mixed with hail, pelting him, stinging him.

Roger tasted mud in his mouth and realized he had fallen without knowing it. His feet were still moving, pushing him through the mire. He tried to stand and couldn't. He was too tired, too weak, the wind was too strong. He crawled to the shelter of a tree.

Currents of rain splashed off the branches and ran in muddy streaks down Roger's face. His left arm was a solid mass of warning spots and the alarm wouldn't stop ringing in his ear. His body was failing and there wasn't anything he could do about it. He feebly attempted to brush a vine away from his face.

One by one his systems were giving up. The tracheal pack in his throat was hopelessly clogged. He was out of nasal filters and his sealant was cracked and torn. Infection or asphyxiation would probably kill him long before he managed to starve to death.

In the canopied branches above his head, the fluffers clung tightly to the trees. He could barely make out their shapes in the dim light. They nestled for protection in the crooks of the larger branches and apparently drew the vines and tendrils of the trees around them. Somehow their presence helped Roger. He didn't feel so alone.

He thought of Teri, of Madge, of Sam. Friends. He drifted in and out of consciousness. It was hard to tell if he was dreaming or awake. Once he thought he saw Teri standing next to him. Another time he thought he saw Sam's pale yellow crystals talking to him in the darkness. He could tell when he cried because his tears were warmer than the rain.

A prolonged flash of chain lightning snapped him awake and provided momentary illumination. What he saw in that drawn-out instant made him wish for the darkness again.

About a meter away from him a fluffer swung

back and forth in the wind. It seemed to be impaled on the branches of the tree. He could have sworn the vines ran straight through the animal's body. One of its legs twitched. Roger closed his eyes. Enough was enough.

Drew Cooper was feeling proud. He'd done a good job, just like he'd been told, and was being complimented for it. Never having received many compliments before, he was a sucker for them.

"I really fixed him, huh?" he said. "Did the trick, right?" They were in a back room off the floater hangar. It was dark and they were alone.

"No sign of him," said the man with him. "You did fine."

"Good. He won't be bothering you no more, I'm sure of that. Ain't nothin' I can't do with a floater. It'll look like an accident even if they find him."

"You're very skillful, Mr. Cooper. We won't forget that." He handed Drew a sealed package.

"What's this?" he asked. "Money?"

"A little something to help you out."

"I would have done it for nothing, you know. Been glad to."

"We know that. Just thought it might come in handy."

Drew nodded, a touch of greed on his face. "It sure will," he said. "It always does."

"How about a little celebration?" asked the man, pulling out a small flask.

"No thanks," said Drew, eyeing it carefully. "I took the vow when I joined the church."

"This is a special occasion. Even the priest has been known to take a nip or two on special occasions."

"No fooling?" asked Drew. "He really does?"

"He told me himself." He unscrewed the cap, passed it to the mechanic.

"I guess a little sip wouldn't hurt none," he said, taking the flask. He chugged half of it. "Good," he said, wiping his mouth with the back of his hand.

Finishing the flask, they sat back in the dark and smoked weedsticks. Drew's was a special one, very potent. It was the strongest one he'd ever had. Also the last. It made him numb all over.

So numb he never felt the knife that killed him.

"Anything you want, you've got," said Jud Walsh. "But I don't see how it's going to help."

"We can't just sit here," said Madge. "I *know* he's alive down there."

"We're doing everything we can. Hundreds of people are combing the planet. The search parties—"

"Damn it, I know all about your search parties. That's not enough. We know how he thinks, what he's likely to do. Besides, if—*when*— you find him he's going to need immediate medical attention, very special attention. It'll have to be me."

"I realize that, Dr. Grinnell. But is there

any real reason for the pilot to go down with you? I would think he would only be in the way."

Madge set her jaw tightly. "He goes," she said, leaving absolutely no room for argument.

"Very well. I suppose you'll need some time to get your equipment ready."

"I've already done that. Get us down there. Now."

"The next scheduled—"

"Screw the schedules. *Now!*"

"Anything you say, Doctor." Walsh shook his head. What a mess. What a goddamn mess.

Madge left his office as quickly as she'd entered. Sam was waiting outside.

"How'd it go?" he signed.

Her hands were a blur. "Grab your toothbrush, old buddy. We're on our way."

Teri walked through a maze of jumbled packing cartons on the loading dock, looking for a floater going out. Hanging around and making a pest of herself seemed to be the best way to get out to look for Roger. She saw three topsiders loading equipment on a large sled and went over to talk to them. As she got closer, she saw that one of them was Henry Sokol.

"If you're going out, Mr. Sokol, can I tag along?" she asked.

He finished tightening a strap holding a large box in place. "It's not up to me," he said. "Not this time, anyway. These people are friends of Roger's. It's their trip."

One of the figures turned around. "You must be Teri," she said. "He talked a lot about you."

"Who? Roger?"

"You were a big help to him. Sure, come along."

Teri pitched in and before long they had the sled loaded. Most of the boxes contained supplies that needed to be delivered to one of the remote bases. Sokol took the controls. Teri strapped herself into the small jump seat behind Madge, squeezing into the space between several cartons. The ground dropped smoothly away as the sled lifted, banking sharply to the left as they headed north.

Teri and Madge hit it off right away. Teri couldn't understand the other one—the one who kept waving his arms around. Madge told her that he was a pilot, but Teri really didn't know what that meant. Madge also told her he was an old friend of Roger's. *That* she could understand. She still couldn't talk to him at all, though, except through Madge. He seemed to be pretty strange.

The volcano had settled down to a steady outpouring of steam and ash. They flew low, covering as much ground as possible. The destruction was complete. Huge trees had been uprooted; they lay like matchsticks, pointing away from the source of the blast. Everything was leveled. There was no sign of Roger or the vehicle he'd been in. Several floaters crisscrossed the area in regular searching patterns.

"If he's there, we'll find him," said Sokol, turning the sled for another pass.

"He's still alive," said Teri, looking out over the ruined landscape. "He's out there somewhere, I can tell. He just has to be."

"Then we'll find him," said Madge.

They looked for five frustrating hours before they dropped off the supplies and returned to the dome.

The rain had stopped, but Roger was far beyond either noticing or caring. His motionless body lay propped against the base of a tree, tangled in a mass of tendrils and vines. The forest was unnaturally quiet, the stillness broken only by the soft rustle of the branches on the wind.

Like bats, or moths in cocoons, the fluffers hung in the trees, swaying slightly with the wind. They were wrapped tightly in twisted balls of vines and tendrils. From a distance they looked like part of the trees themselves; seed pods perhaps, or some strange fruit.

Roger hadn't moved in hours. One unseeing eye, glazed over, was propped half open. His respiration rate was so low he scarcely took a breath every thirty seconds. A large vine had wound itself several times around his body and a spreading web of smaller tendrils covered his burned hands and the side of his face.

Slowly another vine worked its way down the trunk of the tree and started to wind itself around Roger. One of his fingers twitched and he moaned softly. The vine shifted, winding itself still tighter around his unprotected body.

Roger moved fitfully, tossing and turning as far as his vine-encircled body could move. He slipped in and out of a murky dream world where it was impossible for him to tell the real from the imagined.

His body felt detached. When he tried to move his arms and legs they wouldn't respond. His head was trapped in a vise-like grip. Roger's eyes were all he could move. What they saw in their limited field of vision made even less sense to him than anything else.

A fluffer hung in front of him, or at least the body of a fluffer. It couldn't be alive, not any more. Its body had been pierced in a thousand places by the thin tendrils that encased it. At places they ran just under the skin of the animal, raising small ridges in its fur. In other places they seemed to disappear straight into its body. They wrapped tightly around the small animal and were in constant motion, like a ball of coiling green worms.

Roger couldn't take his eyes off the macabre vision; he was drawn to it with an unfocused fascination. It swayed back and forth in the wind, presenting first one side and then the other. The cocoon had a hypnotic effect, like some gruesome watch being dangled in front of him on a very long chain.

Then it opened one eye, one terrible eye.

The white around its iris was tinted a dull green, the same shade of green as the leaves on the trees. Life seemed drained from it. The fluffer stared deeply into Roger's own eyes. Then it blinked.

Roger tried to scream and couldn't. Nothing would work. No sound came from his outraged mouth. His tongue was jammed against a solid object. He gagged.

His mouth was stuffed with something. It had a pulpy taste.

CHAPTER ELEVEN

As Dr. Eric Holmes walked by the double doors to the lab on the orbiting station he had a lot on his mind. The last series of tests hadn't worked out well at all. In particular, the second run-through of the Rockman Intelligence Evaluation had been nothing short of a fiasco. On the first time through, the fluffers had achieved extremely high scores, well up into the eightieth percentile. But that only happened when he was the one who administered the examination. The results were simply not reproducible. If anyone else ran the test the animals didn't score nearly as well. Eric had come back up to the station to regroup and go over the autopsy they'd done on some of the animals that had died.

It was distressing to Eric that so many fluffers died in captivity. Although he didn't keep those that he studied any longer than the short period he needed them, other scientists were working with them on different projects, and the animals had a frighteningly high mortality rate. He suspected that there must be something critical in their normal environment that the experimenters weren't providing, but he'd be damned if he could figure out what it was. As strange as the animals were, it could be almost anything. Nonetheless, they rarely survived much more than an overnight stay. The doors to the lab swung open and a man peeked out.

"Excuse me," he said. "Are you Mr. Trent?"

Eric stopped, confused for a moment by the interrruption of his train of thought. "No," he said. "I'm Dr. Holmes, Eric Holmes."

"Oh, you're the fluffer man. I get your stuff sometimes. I'm looking for this Trent fellow. Thought you might be him. Sorry."

"That's okay," said Eric. "I think he's supposed to be on Frost now."

"Just a small problem. He must have gotten his samples mixed or mislabeled. Something like that, anyway. Just looks a little funny, that's all."

Eric had only met Roger a couple of times. He seemed to be a nice enough fellow, but he really didn't know much about what Roger had been doing.

"I'm afraid I'm not at all that familiar with his work," he said. "We're in different areas. I thought I heard he'd had an accident or something."

"Couldn't prove it by me," said the man. "They never tell me anything. I just run the machines."

The man ducked back into the lab. For a minute Eric thought about following him to see what the problem was, but decided not to. That Trent fellow had been working with the atmosphere.

He didn't have much to do with the fluffers at all.

Roger forced his eyes open, fighting his way back from a bitter nightmare. Somehow he had managed to get some rest, and he'd needed it badly. He felt a little better, and the Bodyguard in his ear had lowered its pitch, which was a good sign. He moved his arm to check on the warning patches Madge had implanted.

As he moved, white powder fell from his arms and forehead. He brushed at it absently, a little annoyed, and then realized it covered his whole body like dust. At first he thought it was ash from the volcano, but it didn't feel like ash. In some places it formed small dusty ridges that crumbled and fell away when he touched them. They looked like dried vines.

The dream came crashing back on him—a warped and twisted recollection, with some parts all too clear—and he jumped to his feet. Frantically he brushed the white powder from his body as if, by removing it, he could shake the memory. There was dust in his mouth, in his eyes, in his ears. In a near frenzy, he spat to get rid of the foul taste, trying to block the images from the night before.

Suddenly he stopped moving and stood perfectly still for a moment. When he had collapsed against the tree he had been nearly dead, yet now he had enough energy to move around. Something had happened. What?

He looked around and noticed the fluffers were on the move again, heading roughly south. There were no dead animals in sight, either on the ground or in the trees. His body ached and he was weak and thirsty, but he started moving along with the animals. It seemed the thing to do. Maybe they knew something he didn't. As he walked, he watched the fluffers with a curious intensity.

"When he gets back I'm going to kill him," said Madge, pacing back and forth. "I've told him a thousand times to let me implant a telemetry unit so I could monitor him from orbit. If he'd let me give him one we could be tracking him now. But no, he wouldn't have one. Invasion of privacy, he said. As if I would snoop on him: *That man!*"

"Glad to see you angry," signed Sam. "Anger is better for you than depression. Much healthier."

"Don't tell me what to feel. Who's the doctor around here, you or me?"

"Ah, anger, I love it. You're beautiful when you get mad."

"Beautiful? I don't have to put up with that kind of—" Madge stopped short and laughed.

"Sorry. I was getting all worked up again. It doesn't help."

"I'll go along with that," signed Sam. He'd been trying to cheer Madge up, maybe shake away some of the gloom that surrounded them. It wasn't doing them any good.

Madge had taken over a room next to the topsiders' clinic on the planet's surface. All her equipment was ready. If they somehow managed to find Roger alive and were able to get him here quickly enough, she could probably help him. Genetically he was a most resilient individual and he healed like a doctor's dream. But they had to find him first and he had to be alive. That was looking increasingly unlikely. Too much time had passed.

But they wouldn't let go, not that easily. They'd held on too long for that.

Henry Sokol walked in and took a seat by Madge's desk. He was their main contact on Frost and they'd seen a lot of him lately.

"They just finished searching the last quadrant of the prime area," he said. "No sign of him. No wreckage, nothing. It looks like he must have gone down with the blow. The timing's right. He could have been there when it went."

"I don't care," said Madge. "He could still be alive."

Sokol shook his head. "I don't think so. If he had simply crashed, the floater's transponder would have been functioning. We'd have picked up his signal by now."

"Maybe it was broken, a malfunction or something."

"You're grasping at straws, Dr. Grinnell. I've never heard of a failure like that. It just doesn't happen. That transponder can stand one hell of a blow, much more than a man could take. There's only one conclusion we can reach."

"You think there's nothing left, right? The transponder's destroyed. The floater's gone, Roger too. Everything blew up, right? Is that what you think?" She was fuming.

"I'm afraid I can't imagine anything else. We have to face facts."

"So you're going to give up on him, is that it? Is that what you're trying to say?" Anger flashed in the woman's eyes. She looked like she was about to hit him.

"No, no," said Sokol, cringing back in the chair. "We'll keep on looking, but you have to be realistic about this. You told me yourself that his support mechanisms would have run out yesterday, even under the best conditions. You've been out there; imagine what it would be like. *Imagine*. He's gone, Dr. Grinnell, admit it."

"I refuse to give up hope," she said desperately. "Not as long as there's the slimmest chance."

"You're only fooling yourself," he said.

Suddenly Madge jumped to her feet. Excitedly, she turned to Sam.

"That's it," she signed. "I completely forgot."

"Forgot what?" asked Sam.

But Madge had run across the room and was digging frantically through a box of her equipment. She had her back turned and didn't see him ask.

Mother Lei was concerned about her daughter. It distressed her to see Teri so overwrought. The girl was tense most of the time, and when she wasn't tense, she was angry. It hurt Lei to watch the child suffer so much, and she tried to help her. But it was an awkward situation, and she wasn't quite sure how to handle it.

"You can't go on like this, always moping around," she said to her daughter. "It isn't healthy. You've done everything you can."

"He's out there somewhere," she muttered, half to herself. "He just has to be."

"I know it's a loss to you, Teri, but you'll just have to get used to it. Life goes on."

"What do you know about loss?" snapped Teri, her eyes flashing. "Or life, either? What have you ever lost that was important to you, as important as this?" To admit the possibility that Roger might be gone was beyond her. In a way it would be admitting that Frost was gone, too; that it would never be hers. It was the loss of a world in more ways than one.

Lei sat quietly and refrained from answering Teri. She knew by now that there was no use in trying to talk with the girl when she was so angry. Still, there *had* been losses in her life, Lei thought to herself. One by one her own mothers had died, soon her sisters would follow suit. Even the dome was dying; soon, it would be empty. The walls of the dome had been her world since childhood, she'd known no other life, had wanted no other world. At times it seemed to Lei that life was nothing more than a long series of losses, one right after the other. Soon, she feared, she would lose her daughter, lose her forever. Flesh of her flesh, the ultimate loss.

Teri sighed and shifted in her chair. Her anger was gone. As usual, it had subsided as quickly as it flared. She looked out the window at the low ground fog around the dome and felt deep embarrassment. Why did she always do this to her mother? Why did her moods swing so quickly?

"He had hopes for Frost," she said quietly. "Great hopes. With his help we could have made it."

"It's a difficult planet," said Lei. "Too much for one man. Too much, maybe, for all of us."

"He could have done it. He could have done almost anything." Her voice was quiet, but even. She spoke with conviction, without doubt.

Lei looked at her daughter and was filled with a sadness that grabbed at her and held her tightly. She wanted things to be good for Teri, but many of those things would be painful for both of them. Teri wanted Frost, a hopeless desire that would tear them apart. Teri wanted Roger alive, which as equally impossible. Wishes, wishes, nothing but dreams. Dreams always turned to ashes.

"Give it up," said Lei. "You have to let go. You'll be happier."

"Let go of what?" asked Teri sharply, snapping her head around. "Let go of Roger? Give up on Frost?"

"That man, what does he mean to you? What can a human *ever* mean to you?"

"He . . . He . . ."

"You're worlds apart. He can't live with you and you can't live with him. You can't even breathe the same air. What good is it? Don't try to tell me you *love* him?" She drew the word out distastefully.

"I don't know," cried Teri in desperation. "He's very special to me. Is that love?"

Lei drew back away from her daughter. Love. She'd never been comfortable with even the word, much less with what it might mean. She guessed she loved her sisters in some way, the same way she had loved her mothers. She thought she loved Teri, but that was somehow different. She had no frames of reference for the experience, nothing to compare it to. For her, love might as well exist in a vacuum, completely internal, feeding upon itself.

"It can't be love," she said finally. "You belong to your people, your flesh and blood. He belongs to his people. It's only natural."

Teri was sobbing openly. "I don't want to hear that," she said through her tears. "I don't believe it. He's a nice person, a kind and good person. I care about him and he cares about me. Maybe that's enough." She straightened up and looked at her mother. "Maybe we just like and respect each other. It could be that's all there ever is to love. I don't know, and I'm sure you don't, either."

That much is true, thought Lei. I *don't* know what love is. I have no idea. I see the sons smile at the daughters and I wonder what it would have been like to have one smile at me that way. She reached out to touch her daughter, to comfort her, but Teri backed away.

It was hard going, but Roger managed to keep up with the fluffers. At times he still wasn't thinking clearly, and more than once he'd found himself circling around and doubling back. It wasn't hard to get confused—everything looked the same. Only by following the animals was he able to keep walking in a straight line.

His mind wandered as he walked. He couldn't understand how he could still be going, why he was still alive. Madge must surely have given up on him by now. Somehow he had the energy to keep moving. When he drank the water he found in small pools it tasted foul but it didn't make him sick. It should have killed him.

The fluffers were a mystery, too. He couldn't have made it without them. Their very survival spurred him on, but there was much more to it than that. Though he couldn't put his finger on it, there was something comforting about the animals. It was almost as if they were calming him, soothing him. Although they stayed in the trees, sliding from branch to branch, it looked like they were moving purposely slower than before, keeping him in sight. It made Roger feel that they cared about him. It was an irrational feeling but he couldn't shake it.

His body continued to ache. He had to stop and rest often. A new pain had been added, a tooth this time. It throbbed for a while and stopped. A few minutes later it started again. He laughed to himself. The situation was too ridiculous for words. Here he was, fighting for his life, and something as minor as a tooth was bothering him. Pain did strange things to your mind.

The tooth! It wasn't an ache at all, but a signal, the alarm Madge had implanted. She used it when she wanted him to check in with her.

In this case, she was using it to show him that they hadn't given up hope, that they still thought he was alive. It lifted his spirits tremendously, and when he started forward again it was with renewed energy. He no longer felt alone.

Even as tired as he was, time passed quickly for Roger. His throbbing tooth was a link to Madge, and it kept him going. His mind was so fogged by fatigue and hunger that when he came across the first mushroom, he didn't recognize it. When he finally realized what it was, the importance of it didn't dawn on him for several minutes.

The mushrooms were terraforming tools, used for specific purposes. They weren't scattered over the planet randomly; they were put in certain places for certain reasons. And they were watched.

He ran into the cleared area, staring open-mouthed at the plants that towered above him. In all his life few things had looked as beautiful as the ugly button-capped fungi. He ran between them, shouting for joy, shouting for someone to hear him.

No one answered. His shouts disappeared into the silence of the mushrooms looming over him. Surrounded by the large plants, he felt suddenly alone again. Their presence was as frightening as it was hopeful. He felt dwarfed, isolated, threatened. The area was deserted.

Roger made his way carefully around the mushrooms, walking slowly now. After a few minutes he came across the remains of an abandoned camp. Two inflatable shelters lay collapsed on the ground. A small tractor lay on its side rusting in a ditch, one tread twisted around the thick roots of a tree. The camp wasn't a currently active one, that much was clear. He looked around for food but couldn't find anything, not even an overlooked flip pak of field rations. Nothing.

A camp like this was never completely abandoned. Someone would be coming by sooner or later to check on things, to monitor the progress of the mushrooms. But that could easily be too late. Hunger gnawed at him continuously. He couldn't afford to wait.

He tried to remove a headlamp from the tractor. With his clumsy injured hands, he cracked it. Working more slowly, he removed the second lens intact.

Roger bunched the two portable shelters together. They were made of lightweight plastic and were easy to move. In the middle he built a small pile of dry twigs and leaves. Using the lens from the tractor he tried to focus the weak rays of the distant sun on the twigs. It took him an hour to get any signs of fire.

He blew gently on it as it smoldered, afraid he might blow it away and have to start over. First a single leaf turned black and curled up. Then another. He shook with nervousness and anticipation, hunched over the smoldering leaves so closely that his nose almost touched the small pile. Another leaf bent with the heat, then some moss sparked into open fire. With shaking hands he dropped some more moss on top, being careful not to smother the small fire. It caught and he pushed a few twigs into it. It grew a little more and he had to move his head back from the heat. A few more larger twigs. Some more moss. It was going!

Then the plastic ignited and it burned with great billowing clouds of thick black smoke. He stepped back with tears in his eyes as he watched the huge acrid cloud rise into the air like a giant smoke signal.

It was almost the end of his shift and the dispatcher was looking forward to his sixteen hours of freetime. He had his eye on that new lady down in data processing. They'd talked on his break, made plans to get together later. It could be interesting; you never knew. The call came in from monitor central.

"Fred, we've got a small burn out by sixty-four nine nine. Nothing serious."

The dispatcher flipped through a loose-leaf book on his desk and punched the intercom open.

"That's a 'room site, isn't it?"

"You got it. An old one."

Fred looked at the master board in front of him. It gave him the approximate locations of all the floaters out in the field.

"Tad and Liz aren't far from there," he said. "I'll send them over to take a look."

"Sounds good. We have them on our screen."

"Probably just another lightning strike," said Fred, closing the book. His relief had just walked in and he was anxious to leave.

"It's probably nothing," said the voice from monitor central. He sounded bored.

CHAPTER TWELVE

A kaleidoscopic nightmare turned over and over in Roger's head. He was running, but quicksand clutched at his feet, dragging him down. Trees loomed over him; fluffers nipped at his body. Everything moved in slow motion; nothing made sense. There were people, voices in the darkness. He slept. It seemed like ages.

He hurt everywhere, but the pain told him he was alive. Eventually he discovered he could move the fingers of one hand. It took him an hour to scratch his nose, longer than that to realize he was floating on an air bed, that the noises he heard were machines keeping him alive.

Faces came and went at irregular intervals. Some seemed familiar, others didn't. They all blurred together. By the time Roger managed to recognize someone, that person had left.

His tongue was thick and swollen. More than anything else, he was overpoweringly thirsty. He was only given occasional slivers of ice to suck on. It was never enough. What he wanted was water, gallons of water. He drifted in and out of consciousness, never really sure if he was awake or not.

Eventually more feeling came back, and with it more pain. He regained a little movement. It may have taken days, weeks. It was all the same to Roger, an endless fog.

A face came by, a familiar face.

"Madge." His voice was barely more than a whisper.

She stopped what she was doing and stared at Roger, not sure she had really heard him speak.

"Madge." It took every bit of energy he had.

"So," she said, relief spreading across her face. "You finally decided to rejoin the land of the living. It's about time."

"I . . ."

"Don't talk. You'll mess up all my work."

Roger closed his eyes and sighed. The same old Madge.

"You've got a lot of healing in front of you," she said. "I had to do a total rebuild on your throat—and damn it, Roger, you should have seen your lungs. They were hard as rocks. It wasn't enough that you had been sightseeing for days with clogged filters, but when they picked you up you were dancing like some crazy man in the thickest mass of roasting hydrocarbons I've ever seen. That alone should have done you in."

"I . . ."

"Shut up. I'm not through bitching yet. Just because you have the constitution of a bull elephant doesn't mean you have to keep trying to prove it. You had us all half out of our minds with worry."

"Teri?"

"Teri's fine, which is more than I can say about you. She was pretty upset. Seems like a nice kid."

Madge turned her back and made some adjustments to his life support system. She felt the tensions of the last few days slipping away from her. He was going to make it. Not that his problems were over yet, but at least he was on the right track.

There was that other thing, though. She had to tell him. As much as she'd like to put it off, she couldn't. It wouldn't be fair. He'd need time to think things over.

"That was close, Roger," she said softly, her voice subdued. "Too damn close." She sat by the side of the bed.

He nodded. It was the barest of motions.

Madge sat stiffly on the edge of the chair. "I've got something to tell you, Roger," she said. "This may not be the best time, but it can't wait. At least you can't give me any back-talk. Not this time." She managed a nervous grin.

"You should be dead," she said. "You were out too long and under too much stress. Most of your support systems were failing or had already gone. By all rights you should have died days ago. Something happened to you out there, something strange. We're not sure of the details yet, but one thing's clear. Whatever it was, it saved your life." She paused and looked at Roger.

"Somehow your body started adjusting to Frost," she said. Roger's eyes locked onto hers.

"It's as simple and as complicated as that. We know a little bit about what's happening to you, but we have no idea how it started. The lab's been running tests constantly, but we're still in the dark."

Roger tried to talk, but his tongue kept getting tangled up. He quit trying.

"I was only half kidding about your lungs. They *were* a mess, but more like wood than stone, packed tightly enough to form a pretty effective filter network. The biopsy confirmed the presence of plant fibers. It's not just your lungs, either. Your whole body has undergone changes, some minor, some pretty major. It seems like a lot to happen in such a short period of time. Some of your basic metabolic pathways have shifted. Your scrapes are healing, but the patches of new skin have a lot of cellulose fibers. Your body seems to be fighting to stay on Frost, even if it has to turn into a plant to do it." She sat back in the chair, absently adjusting the flow rate of one of his meds. It had started to drift.

"I'm not kidding, Roger. Something strange has happened to you and we don't know if a factor on the planet caused it or if it's an aspect of your body we haven't seen before. Whatever it is, it gives us a problem." She looked away from him for a moment. This was hard.

"You're hanging in the balance right now, Roger. Not between life and death, but between Frost and Earth. You could literally go either way. As soon as you're a little stronger, I'll finish patching you up. But you'll have to tell me which way to go, Earth or Frost. Before you decide, there are a couple more things you ought to know.

"If we put you back to Earth-normal you can't ever go back out on Frost again. We can't take the chance of triggering this effect again. That's the easy half.

"Completing your adaptation to Frost would be more difficult, but not impossible. There are two catches to it, though. One is that it would be irreversible; you'd never be able to change back. The other is that you'd be dead within two years unless Frost stabilizes."

She reached out and took his hand. "Do you understand me?" she asked. "Squeeze my hand if you understand."

The pressure was faint, but unmistakable.

"We're glad to have you back, Roger," she said. "I wasn't sure I'd ever see you again."

Roger looked at her hand. It seemed so soft against his scarred and bandaged one. Then he looked into her face, her eyes. He thought he saw tears, but that wasn't possible. Madge *never* cried.

* * *

Morris Twelve knelt in the darkness of the meditation room with his eyes tightly closed. He, too, was filled with pain. His pain was a tortured mixture of anger and sorrow.

Drew Seven had been killed, his body discovered down on that terrible planet. His death touched Morris deeply, affecting him in ways he'd never known before. He had brought Drew into the Church of the One True Way and that had established a special bond between the two men.

Drew had been killed by strangers, but his death would always be on Morris's hands, as his life had been. Bringing another person into the church was not a matter to be taken lightly. Morris had pledged at the time to help guide Drew's development in every possible way. It was a serious vow.

The death stung, as if his own brother had died. Drew's murder would not be forgotten, not as long as Morris continued to draw breath. He would pledge the rest of his life for good works in Drew's memory, and if the opportunity came to avenge his death, Morris would not hesitate to do so.

He clenched his fists and tried to push the anger down, but it wouldn't leave him. It settled in his gut like a hard knot of hate. There was no serenity here, no quiet pastures. He felt only turmoil.

Drew had been rescued from a life of sin, a life that would have dragged him down. He had finally seen the light, but to what avail?

He had hardly begun to live the right life, the One True Way. He'd had no time. It was cruel, unfair.

Morris thought how far he had come from those simple times back on Paragon. It seemed almost like a dream to him now. The daily routines and small details that had made up his life back on that planet seemed blurred and far away. It was almost as if they had happened to someone else, or had been a story he'd once seen on the vid. His life since then had become complicated, far beyond anything he'd expected. It was good to serve the church, but he had doubts that he was up to it. Maybe they had chosen the wrong man. There were so many setbacks.

And now there was this death to contend with. It was not a simple matter. Rituals had to be done, things needed to be prepared. And then there was the hate, hate for an unknown person, an unknown face. Nothing was simple anymore.

At least the priest was nearby during these terrible times. His words often comforted Morris. The man was a saint. He knew how to lift worries and burdens with a few well-chosen phrases. He felt the priest was one of the universe's few truly good men.

He would do anything for him.

They talked in the darkness of a storage room on the orbiting station, keeping to the shadows so they wouldn't be seen together.

That could only bring trouble. The priest was used to the shadows, the other man wasn't.

"It didn't work." The priest's words were simple and direct, his voice full of anger.

"I know, I know. It's not my fault. He should have been dead ten times over. You almost have to admire his stamina."

"I don't have to admire anything about him."

"Sorry."

"You ought to be," he snapped. "It wasn't that complicated. I would have thought you could handle it."

"How was I supposed to know he'd last that long?"

"You're supposed to know everything down there. That's your job."

"It can't be traced. The mechanic has been taken care of. I did it myself. No one else knew. We're clean."

"So now we try again," said the priest. "Or, rather, *you* try again."

"Me? Wait a minute."

"The word's just come down. They made a decision at the highest level. It's not supposed to look like an accident this time."

"What? I thought—"

"You think too much, usually. Sometimes you don't think enough. They want this one traced to the chimeras."

"You're kidding. That's crazy."

"See what I mean? You don't think things through. It makes good sense. Imagine what would happen if a chimera was to kill a man. People would go wild. At the very least it would stop the project cold, and that's what they want."

"But why would they want to kill him? They all like him, think he's some sort of a god. He wants to help them. No, it wouldn't work."

"Suppose he had discovered that Frost could never be changed enough for them. Wouldn't that make them mad? Mad enough to kill him?"

"But he hasn't discovered anything of the sort."

"Use your head. Set it up."

"Is that *all*?" asked the man.

"Don't get smart with me," snapped the priest. "Just do it."

He watched the man leave. It was a shame they didn't have any more of the faithful on the planet's surface. They owned this man through his wallet. That wasn't nearly as good as owning them through their souls.

Roger gradually got used to the noises, the dull pain, the nurses and doctors who came and went at regular intervals. What he couldn't get used to was the confinement and the time he was wasting while recovering. He felt his body had let him down. It was frustrating. He was a terrible patient, always complaining.

Sam had just left. At least they allowed him occasional visitors. That helped some. Without being able to move his arms much, he'd had trouble talking with Sam. Fingerspelling took too long. He'd tried whispering, knowing that Sam could read his lips. It seemed to be a selective ability, though. Every time he'd started griping, Sam would sign that he couldn't understand.

Still, it was good to see him, and the visit had lifted his spirits for a little while. Sam was good at that—it was one of his major talents. But soon after he'd left, the same old depressions started settling in, the same old frustrations and worries. He wanted to get back to work so he could drive some of these concerns away.

Roger had been in and out of the operating room so many times he'd lost count. That really didn't bother him too much. It had been a part of his life for many years and he trusted Madge more than any other person he knew. She'd pretty well stabilized him. The rest was waiting out the recovery process. He was still a little upset over the transducer Madge had implanted, the one that monitored his health. He knew she'd put it in with the best of intentions, but she'd done it over his protests. It gave him the feeling that someone was watching over him all the time like a mother hen. He was too old for that. The chances he took ought to be of his own choosing.

But some of the other choices weren't so easy. He hung in limbo, halfway between Earth and Frost. Madge could keep him there for a while, but it was a decision he'd have to make sooner or later. It wasn't going to be an easy one. This planet had already shown him a lot about life, about death, about survival. Then there was Teri and her people. He owed them something; a finished job, a planet they could live on. His feelings were complicated, diffuse, hard to get a handle on or come to terms with. It wasn't like a profit-loss ledger sheet where items lined up neatly in one column or another. There was a lot he didn't understand yet; about the planet, about himself.

Someone moved past the small window to his room, just at the edge of his vision. He couldn't see who it was. It happened all the time: doctors checking up on him, nurses, people just passing by who wanted to see what kind of a monster could have survived out there so long.

Monster. He didn't feel like a monster. He felt more like a man just trying to do his job, a man betrayed by his own body.

He thought of the other planets he'd worked on. Some of them had been harsh, some benign. They had all been beautiful in one way or another. There was beauty everywhere if you took the time to look for it. He thought of Earth and his home by the sea, the home he loved but never had enough time for. If he opted for Frost all that would be gone. All the other planets, past and future, would be gone too. There would be no more strange worlds under alien suns, each with their own unique problems to be worked out. And he would be paying with his life, too. But what good was a life except for what you did with it? On the other hand, what could he hope to accomplish in two years on Frost? It was a heavy price to pay and he wasn't even sure what he'd be paying it for. Pride? The challenge of beating Frost? Teri?

There had to be reasons, factors he couldn't quite grasp, or he wouldn't even be considering the change. But he wasn't sure he could flip the other way, either, and turn his back on Frost, on Teri and her people. There were no easy answers.

Another figure moved past the window, or maybe it was the same one. Roger tried to move his head to see, but it hurt too much. He cursed his body and closed his eyes, trying to find answers to questions he didn't even understand.

Madge and Teri faced each other, separated by a thick plate window of quartz. Madge was on the inside, Teri on the outside. They spoke through microphones. They were inches apart, worlds apart.

"How's he doing today?" asked Teri, flushing immediately. She always asked the same questions, day after day. She was worried that Madge would tire of her constant visits.

"Better all the time," said Madge. "Not exactly kicking up his heels yet, but he's improving." She was tired from the long hours she'd been putting in, but it was good to see Teri. There was something fresh about her, something touching about her concern for Roger.

Although Teri was hardly more than a child—a young adult, to be more precise—Madge saw that in many ways she was much older than her years would indicate. The hope she held for Roger seemed at times to be like a child's hope, a simple wish that he would get well and set her world right. On other levels, though, there were other concerns, adult concerns. Teri was growing up fast, caught between two worlds.

"I . . . we were wondering when he could have visitors," asked Teri.

Madge laughed. "You mean, when will *you* be able to see him."

Teri looked away shyly and nodded.

It was hard for Madge not to smile. The girl/woman was so open and honest, almost transparent at times. Teri's people hadn't yet learned the so-called social graces that involved casual lying and evasiveness. She had complexities of a different sort. She'd need them to survive on Frost, providing the situation ever came to pass.

A tough road lay ahead for these people. Madge felt for them. She'd been through some pretty rough times herself, and knew a little of how they must feel. She liked Teri, who could be soft one minute and hard as a rock the next. She'd make it if any of them could.

"I think it could be arranged," she said. "It might take a while to set things up, though."

"Do you really think so?" asked Teri, her eyes lighting up with hope. "*Me?*"

Madge felt something crack within the hard shell she imagined she carried inside herself. Teri felt so much, and she didn't hide anything. It was almost painful to watch, but beautiful.

"I'll set it up," she said.

"Thank you, Dr. Grinnell," said Teri with tears in her eyes. "Thank you." She placed her hand up against the quartz plate glass.

Madge reached up and placed her hand by Teri's. The thick, insulated glass separated them, but it seemed much less than that. It was impossible, but the glass felt warmer to Madge, as if they were actually touching. Something passed between them, something no machine could measure. She wanted to reach through the quartz and hug the girl, to try and show her how much she understood.

"Call me Madge," she said. "We're friends."

"Friends," echoed Teri and her smile was so infectious it caught Madge up and carried her to places she hadn't been in a long time.

Eric had gone over the data thoroughly. He'd even had his two assistants run through the entire battery of tests again with different animals. The results were fine whenever there wasn't a skeptic around, but as soon as he tried to demonstrate it to any of the representatives of Unity Alliance, the animals failed to perform. It didn't make any sense.

It was almost as if the tests were rigged,

which Eric knew wasn't the case. Sometimes he got the feeling that the animals sensed their anxiety, their hope that the fluffers would turn out to be intelligent creatures. But that was ridiculous, too. He had checked that aspect of the tests very carefully. The suits they wore while working with the fluffers precluded the use of facial gestures and most body language as visible cues for the animals. The experimenters had been filmed along with the fluffers in all the tests, and not once had any movement shown up that would have given the animals a clue. Even the people from Unity admitted that when they reviewed the tapes. But they suspected other trickery, perhaps off-camera. Eric knew there wasn't any trickery. Proving it was another matter.

There was a possible way around the problem. If Eric could find a totally unbiased individual to run the experiment it would eliminate any unconscious cues that might be slipping through. However, finding someone around Frost who didn't have a vested interest in the fluffers would be hard. Almost everyone in the area had something at stake with the animals one way or another. He'd look into it, though. Something had to be done.

He shuffled through the stack of lab reports on his desk. Eric was going back to the planet's surface in a few hours and wanted to make sure he'd caught up on everything. Several additional autopsy reports on the fluffers had come in and did nothing but complicate the picture. It seemed like the animals had more individual differences than similarities. How one species of animal could have so much variation was beyond him. He wouldn't be too surprised to pick up a form one day and read something like: "This individual was a silicon-based organism who exhaled methane while metabolizing materials primarily composed of granite." That was stretching the point, but not by much. They were strange creatures.

But, then, the whole planet was strange.

One of the folders on his desk had been given to him by mistake. It belonged to Roger Trent. Eric was vaguely aware that Roger had been lost for a while, then found. He didn't know any details. He'd heard that Roger wasn't going anywhere for a while, that the doctor he'd brought along was replacing kidneys and such right and left. Idly, Eric opened the folder and flipped through the flimsy papers with mild curiosity. He recalled that Trent had been working with the atmosphere. It couldn't have much to do with his investigations.

As he was flipping it closed, the word *fluffer* caught his eye. Anything that had to do with the animals usually drew his attention. The report said sample number 0073/RT527 was— according to the notation—a seed that had been buried by a fluffer. The date and location had been carefully noted. The next sample, number 0073/RT528, was labeled as a seed removed from the same tree by Roger, untouched by a fluffer. The chemical analysis of the two seeds showed marked differences; even he, not being a chemist, could see that. But what did it mean? It was probably nothing. If the trees were half as varied as the fluffers, anything was possible. He closed the folder and re-routed it back to the lab. It would eventually find its way back to Roger.

It looked like pretty routine stuff, probably not important.

It was difficult to get Teri in to see Roger, but they finally managed. Short of getting him out to see her, there was no way they could calm either one of them down. They chose the slightly less complicated path.

Roger's room had been anything but the quiet recovery area it was supposed to be. Visitors came constantly and at all hours. Sam nearly had to be pried off his chair. His bedside watch had begun during Roger's surgery and he had refused to leave until he was sure his boss was out of danger.

In spite of Madge's protests, Roger had insisted on dragging in experts on Frost and picking their brains. The room was a madhouse most of the time, and Roger refused to slack off. As weak as he was, he was also a man possessed. He wanted answers. Madge tried to keep the visits short, but that was the best she could hope for and she rarely succeeded.

Teri wore a modified crisis bag, a multipurpose garment designed for use in the shuttle. Transparent and bulky, it was used to protect workers in emergency situations. One size fit everybody. An umbilical cord had been rigged to supply her with an appropriate atmosphere. Henry Sokol helped her maneuver through the door into Roger's room. It was a complicated procedure.

He looked worse than she'd expected. Somehow, Roger had always seemed a little bigger than life to her, and although she was prepared to see him sick, she hadn't expected it to be this bad.

The left side of his body was enclosed in a transparent cast. Underneath the cast his skin grafts were angry red patches. Tubes slid into his free arm, his nose, his mouth. The room was filled with soft gurgling and whirring noises. His face was a patchwork quilt of surgical scars in the process of healing; his throat was a mess. He looked terrible.

"It's good to see you," said Teri softly. She stopped at the foot of the bed, standing there awkwardly. She was nervous, afraid to come any closer. A large part of her wanted to run to him, touch him, reassure herself that he still lived. More than the suit she wore held her back. He looked so fragile.

Sokol walked to the far side of the room and sat on a bench by the monitoring system, allowing the two of them to have this time more or less to themselves. He studied the equipment with interest.

"Sorry we missed the trip to the ocean," said Roger, forming the words with difficulty.

"We'll make it some other time, I promise you. Soon."

"I—we were worried," she said. "I looked all over for you."

"I know. Madge told me."

"I like Madge. Is she your special friend? I mean, uh, you know, *special*, like a lover?"

Roger almost laughed. "She's a friend, and she's certainly special, but a lover? No, I don't think so, not the way you mean. Sometimes I get the idea she doesn't even like me very much. She sure spends a lot of her time making me uncomfortable." He moved his right arm, waving the tubes around.

"How is the farm doing?" asked Roger.

Her face brightened up. "We've gained almost five more square kilometers," she said. "And the latest crop of bytome has lasted twice as long as any of the others. Things look good." It hadn't been *that* good. She was trying to cheer up Roger.

"If we didn't have to fight the trees all the time, we'd really be getting somewhere."

Trees. The mention of them sent involuntary shudders up and down Roger's spine. The uneasy dreams were never far from the surface these days.

"Are the fluffers still around, Teri?"

"Sure. They're always out there somewhere."

"Do you know where they sleep?"

"In the forest, I guess. They go into the woods every night."

"Have you actually seen them? I mean, has

anyone ever followed them to watch them sleep?"

She shrugged, a gesture she'd picked up from him. "I don't know. Why would anyone want to watch a fluffer sleep? They go pretty far back into the forest. There wouldn't be any reason to follow them."

"I want to ask you to do me a favor, Teri," he said.

"Sure."

"See if you can find out where they sleep and how they sleep."

"I'll try, but they always run away from me. Maybe it'll be different after dark."

"Run away?"

"I've always thought they were scared of us or something. When they see me coming across the field they go the other way."

That was strange. They'd never shown any reaction at all to Roger, neither fear nor aggression. Most of the time they'd simply ignored him. Except once.

"One more thing, Teri. Take someone with you. Don't go alone."

There was something in his voice when he spoke that frightened Teri.

"I understand," she said. "I'm sure Lan will come with me."

"Fine. Just be careful."

"Time to go, Teri," said Sokol. "The doctor told me you could stay two minutes and it's been more than five. We'd better leave before we wear him out."

"Wait, Henry," said Roger. "I want you to do something for me, too."

"What's that, Mr. Trent?"

"I want to see everything you have on the fluffers."

"That's impossible," he said. "Even if you were well enough to work it couldn't be done. There's just too much data on the animals. The summary sheets alone would fill this room."

"I don't want summary sheets and I'm not interested in abstracts. I want *everything*, all the raw information. Surely it's all filed somewhere, isn't it?"

"Of course. It's all in the master datanet."

"Then I must have a terminal in this room and the proper access codes. I'll need data on the trees, too."

"There's too much stored in there, and it's all jumbled up. You'll never be able to sort it all out."

"Let me be the judge of that, Henry. That's what you pay me for. Just get me the terminal and the codes. I'll worry about the rest."

"I think you're wasting your time with this. Besides, you can hardly move, and—"

"Get them! I want to start this afternoon."

"Whatever you say, Mr. Trent. We'd better leave, Teri."

"I'll be back to see you as soon as they let me," she said. There was more she wanted to say, much more, but the words were buried deeply and she couldn't get them out.

"Take care of yourself, Teri."

"You, too," she said as they left.

Alone in his room, Roger tried to sort out what connections he was looking for. He didn't know, exactly, but that didn't bother him. It was just the way he worked. Something vague would bother him and he'd mess around with whatever information he had until the pieces started to fall into place. It was a strange way of working, but he had grown accustomed to it over the years.

The trees had something to do with it, beyond a doubt, and the fluffers had something to do with the trees. There were connections there, and it was all tied up with what had happened to him while he was out in the forest.

He coughed. The lights in the room were dim. He felt a little lightheaded. Maybe Madge was right. He'd been pressing himself pretty hard.

He couldn't help it. There was so much to do and so little time. There were questions he had to find answers to, decisions he had to make.

He coughed again, and when he tried to catch his breath no air came. His lungs heaved, but nothing happened. He clutched blindly at the tubes that ran through his nose. Reaching for the button to call the nurse, his eyes glazed over and he fell out of bed.

In the dim room, no one saw him fall, no

one heard the noise. The alarms on the monitors were strangely silent.

He jerked on the floor for a moment and then lay still.

CHAPTER THIRTEEN

Madge sat up with a jolt, knocking over her coffee cup. It couldn't be. *No, not that!* She threw her chair back and ran into the next room. The small black box sat on her workbench, test leads still hooked up. She hadn't finished calibrating it yet, but it was working. For a moment she stood staring at it, transfixed. It was beeping, and a red light was flashing. *Damn.* She turned and ran from her room.

Sprinting down the corridor, she kicked open the door to the monitoring room. The nurse sat at his station, his nose buried in a stack of papers scattered all over the desk. He was daydreaming and seemed to be almost asleep. Startled, he looked up.

"What's happening?" he asked. Madge was already halfway across the room.

"Damn it, *move!*" The alarms in the monitoring room were silent. She pushed open Roger's door, hoping to find him sitting in bed, hoping that the whole thing was a mistake. She saw him lying on the floor. His skin was pale, with a faint bluish tint. Cyanotic: oxygen deprivation. Have to move fast. She dropped down beside him.

"Give me—"

"Here it is," said the nurse, handing her the portable oxygen.

Madge's hands trembled slightly as she made the connection. Her professionalism was slipping. Roger was slipping. She tightened the clamps with a twist and turned the oxygen up full.

As the gas hissed, Madge's eyes darted around the room gathering details. Roger's oxygen supply had been cut off at the wall. The thing that made it serious was that Roger's normal breathing responses had been blocked by medication while he was being fed a special mixture of oxygen, Earth's atmosphere, and Frost's contaminates.

Roger started to move, first with a faint twitching of his fingers, and then more strongly. His arms thrashed wildly, aimlessly.

The nurse took Roger's arms and pinned them to the floor. Madge glared at the young man. Was it his mistake that had caused all this? His eyes were full of fear. If he'd done anything, he was hiding it well. He looked scared, surprised.

Roger's color was coming back. He strained against the nurse, fighting him. His eyes opened, but they were distant, and unfocused. He tried to grab the oxygen. Madge gently moved his hand back.

"Did you unhook him?" asked Madge.

"No, never," said the nurse, shaking his head.

"What about the last time you suctioned him?"

"I don't work that way, Dr. Grinnell, honest, I don't."

Madge eyed him closely. He seemed to be telling the truth. She didn't think he knew what had happened.

Two things had gone wrong that shouldn't have. His oxygen line had somehow come loose, and with the bayonet coupling that shouldn't have happened. No way.

In itself, that wouldn't have been so bad if the regular bedside alarm had gone off and notified the nurse. For some reason it had been switched over to standby mode and hadn't rung. Unfortunately, that did happen occasionally.

Patients in Roger's condition were surrounded by a complicated system of wires. Everything was continually monitored, measured, and checked to see that certain vital functions never exceeded or fell below carefully set limits. Moving a patient in his bed, or suctioning—which had to be done several times a day—made the monitoring system go crazy. Wires crossed each other, leads touched, interfering with readings. The false values made the alarms go off. As a matter of convenience, nurses often set the monitors to standby mode when they had to move the patients. That way the alarms didn't sound. Once in a while they forgot to turn them back on. It didn't happen often, but it happened.

Roger moaned, looked around. His eyes were starting to focus. He was coming out of it. Madge relaxed a little and leaned over him.

"You lead a charmed life, old friend," she said. He reached out to her and she took his hand. "If I hadn't implanted that remote telemeter we'd be digging you a hole right now." She resisted an urge to lecture him on his stubbornness. He'd been through enough.

"As it is, we'll just have to drag you back up on the bed. I hope you've lost some weight." She made light of it, but it had been a near thing. It was a setback, probably minor, but it could have been much worse. She shuddered.

As they moved Roger, the nurse swore he hadn't touched either the alarms or the oxygen. Madge wanted to believe him—he seemed so sincere, so frightened—but she really didn't know what to think.

The priest glared across the small table at Henry Sokol. They sat on pillows in one of the cubicles screened off in the pleasure room of the orbiting station. The lights were subdued and the smell of weed was heavy in the air.

"Two failures," he said. "That's two more than you're allowed."

"I couldn't help it. How was I supposed to know the doctor had put that thing in him?"

"Excuses," snapped the priest. "I don't want to hear excuses. Do you think that makes any difference to them? They want results, not words."

"But it wasn't my fault!"

"Keep your voice down," said the priest, leaning over to raise the volume on the music piped into the cubicle. "Anyway, your stupidity has changed the picture."

"Changed? How?"

"They want him dead, and they want him dead *now*. They don't care what it looks like as long as he's dead. Making it look like the chimeras did it would be nice, but it's no longer very important. I guess they think he's close to something."

"I was trying to frame a certain chimera. She's trouble anyway, and it would be good to get rid of her. She'd be a natural, since she has a hot temper."

"They don't want to wait. It has to be right now."

Sokol twisted nervously, pulling at the fringe on his pillow. Fear welled up inside of him. It was a familiar feeling. He couldn't remember when he hadn't felt it. He was helpless, caught in the interlocking gears of a power struggle so vast and complex that he saw only the edges of it. Powerful forces were trying to wrest control of Frost away from Unity, and people like himself were expendable.

The priest was just one small part of a much larger operation. Sokol suspected that the man was being used and manipulated the same way he was. They were all caught up in the same web. The only difference was that some of them could move a little more than others.

He'd started out doing small favors for faceless individuals, supplying them with trivial information in return for substantial cash. Later he'd tapped into the datanet, manipulating certain key factors. Once the misinformation had been integrated into the system, it was accepted as fact by anyone who used it. Each step had tangled him up a little more. Before he knew it, he was in too far. He was trapped.

He couldn't believe how deeply he'd been sucked into everything. Murder. Genocide. Would there never be an end to this? All he knew for sure was that there was no turning back. Like the unfortunate Drew, he knew too much. Far too much.

"I think they suspect something," he said. "It won't be easy. There's someone with him all the time."

"That's your problem," said the priest. "Just get the job done."

Sokol nodded grimly. He understood perfectly. This was his last chance.

The black branches swayed rhythmically above them, thin fingers silhouetted against the rapidly darkening sky. The wind moaned constantly. Teri and Lan moved a little closer together for mutual support.

They sat under a crude shelter made of old branches at the base of a large tree. It seemed like they'd been there forever, but it had only been a couple of hours. Nightfall came quickly in the forest.

"It's spooky in here," said Lan. "What exactly are we looking for, anyway?"

"I don't know," said Teri. "Roger didn't say. We're supposed to see what the fluffers do at night, I guess."

Teri was more shaken than she cared to admit. It was scary this far into the forest at night. This was the first time any of them had been this deep into the woods after dark. Even with Lan beside her, she felt alone. She couldn't shake the feeling that she was someplace she didn't belong, doing something she shouldn't be doing. When they spoke it was in hushed whispers.

Time passed slowly. The darkness settled around them like a dark, damp blanket. Each small noise brought a jolt of fear to their hearts. By the time the first fluffers came, Lan was a nervous wreck and Teri wasn't much better. They heard the animals before they saw them, a faint chittering in the upper branches of the trees.

"Look," whispered Teri, pointing almost directly overhead.

Two fluffers were moving slowly through the interlocking branches, carefully picking their way to the trunk of the tree. They settled down in a large fork and made soft clicking noises deep in their throats, noises that Teri had never heard before. The animals were facing the trunk of the tree and caressed the bark as they made the strange sounds. It was eerie, almost as if the fluffers were talking with the tree.

"What are they doing?" asked Lan, his curiosity pushing the fear back just a little.

"I don't have any idea," said Teri. Whatever it was, she didn't like the looks of it.

The small animals reached around where they stood, gathering the strands of vines that hung from the tree like Spanish moss. They wrapped the vines around themselves in tight coils.

Teri and Lan suddenly realized that this scene was being duplicated all around them. There were maybe a dozen fluffers within view and they were all in various stages of wrapping themselves in the loosely hanging vines. The fiber-like tendrils were everywhere.

"I'm going to get a better look," said Teri, starting to move away from their shelter.

"Where are you going?" asked Lan, fear making his voice too loud. He grabbed her arm. "Don't leave me here."

"I'm just going over there," she said, pointing at a fluffer hanging from a nearby tree. "I want to see what it looks like up close. It's hard to see much in the dark."

"I'm coming with you," he said.

"Suit yourself. There's nothing to be afraid of." She didn't feel as brave as she sounded. "They're just fluffers," she said.

Somehow, that didn't ease Lan's mind at all.

This particular fluffer had chosen a lower

branch and was hanging about eye level, swinging back and forth. At first glance it looked like the animal had wrapped the vines around itself like a blanket. Up close, it looked different. Much different.

The vines that encased the fluffer were slowly churning. The cocoon was a dark, writhing mass, seemingly alive. With horror, Terri saw that the fluffer's body was pierced in a hundred places and that the vines slid in and out of the helpless animal like burrowing leeches. Her stomach gave a sickening wrench and she gagged. Lan screamed: it sounded far away, empty and hollow. Then she saw it, too. The animal was still alive. It breathed slowly, watching them with dull eyes that held only the barest spark of life, eyes from which small tendrils were sprouting even as they watched. A vine suddenly erupted from the fluffer's belly. Bits of flesh sprayed them both. There was no blood.

Her scream joined Lan's as they ran stumbling through the threatening darkness back to the dome.

Roger's room was a mess. Computer flimsies covered almost every flat surface, including the walls. Only a small space on the bed and an area near the computer terminal were clear. He hobbled around the room, muttering quietly to himself as he paced the floor, carefully avoiding the stacks of printouts that seemed to be everywhere.

He was upset, mad at himself for taking so

long to recover. Nothing like this had ever happened before. Usually he was up and around in a matter of hours. The fact that he'd been through a rough time didn't seem like a reasonable excuse to him. There'd been other rough times. It was as if his body had let him down.

He swept some papers off the chair and sat down in front of the terminal. At least they'd managed to get that to him, even though he'd had to keep prodding them. For the last few days he'd been working with it, getting to know his way around. Using the terminal was easy. Sorting out the data was the hard part. Sokol had been right, there was a *lot* of information in there, much of it contradictory.

There were two ways to use the datanet; one easy, one hard. The easy way was direct and simple. It had to be that way because most of the people who used the datanet were scientists and researchers of various sorts, not computer programmers. These people had neither the time nor, often, the skills necessary to learn the details of computer operation. The system was designed so that they could ask questions in simple language and get back answers they could understand.

The more complex way into the datanet was primarily used by the computer people to perform internal manipulations. It was a complicated language, full of seemingly meaningless groups of letters and numbers. Roger found a certain logic to it, though, and after a couple evenings of study he had a fair handle on it. That was when his work really started.

He began with the fluffers, not trying to follow any one thing in particular. He'd scanned randomly, letting it all flow past him. Occasionally he would pick up on the hint of a pattern and follow it for a while, only to drift off later in another direction. He let his subconscious do most of the work.

It was often this way when he started a new phase of an investigation. He was just getting a feel for it, developing a system for using the terminal so that it became natural. A lot of the data he was looking at reinforced the observations he'd had in the field. Some of it didn't, though, and that bothered him. Where there were discrepancies, he tried moving things around to make all the pieces fit. Sometimes they didn't fit, no matter what he did. He was punching up a new screen when Madge came in.

"How's my grumpy patient today?" she asked.

"Messing," he said, scanning the numbers. "Mucking around."

"What's new? You're always messing."

"No, not me. Somebody else."

"I don't understand. What do you mean?"

"Somebody's been manipulating the datanet. Look at this." He punched up the query screen and asked for the atmospheric concentration of sulphur dioxide for a day two weeks ago. A number flashed instantly on the screen.

"So?" said Madge.

"That number is what the datanet recognizes as the average concentration of sulphur dioxide for that day. It's pretty high, but that's not the only problem." He called back the query screen and started punching in a long stream of numbers, occasionally stopping to refer to a checklist taped to the side of the terminal.

"Sulphur dioxide concentration isn't uniform through the atmosphere. Some places have more of it than others, so what the datanet gave us was an average value. This number was based on figures reported from both ground-based monitoring stations and satellites. There are over two hudred stations and almost that many satellites. It's a lot of raw data."

Numbers started sliding across the screen. There seemed to be no end to them.

"What I've just done is tap into the raw data as supplied by the monitors. Most people wouldn't go this far into the datanet. Usually, there's no reason to."

"So why did you?" asked Madge.

"Just a hunch. Things didn't feel right. So I took the raw data and did my own calculations. The figure I get is much lower than the one I just showed you."

"So it made a mistake. Big deal."

"It *didn't* make a mistake, that's the whole point. It gave the figure it was told to give. But it was told to give the wrong numbers. Somebody wanted it to do that."

"It looks pretty complicated," said Madge. "It could have been an honest mistake."

"No. I thought it might be, at first, but it happens throughout the datanet. A series of measurements shows that a particular glacier is advancing, but I know it's receding. I've seen it with my own eyes. Even data I gathered and entered myself has been changed. Someone's been tampering with the datanet."

"Why would anyone want to do that?"

"To create confusion," said Roger. "If a biologist, for example, wants to know something about the chemistry of the ocean, the first thing he does is go to the datanet. It would never occur to him that the computer might lie to him. He accepts what it tells him as fact, and proceeds from there. Working with false assumptions, his research is bound to go off on a tangent, affecting other people's work. It spreads like ripples in a pond, only faster. Soon everything is working at cross purposes and you've got a royal mess. It's amazing how few pieces of misinformation it takes to throw the whole project off track. Somebody wants Unity to fail, and they want it badly."

"Who?"

"Take your pick. A lot of people would love to see it happen."

"Ecofreaks? Fanatics?"

"I don't think so. This feels like something bigger. It could be someone who'd like to step in and pick up the pieces that Unity would leave behind. It could be another corporation, maybe. Frost is an extremely valuable planet."

"I . . ." Madge paused. "I never believed that loose oxygen coupling was an accident."

"And I don't think the floater was an accident, either," said Roger. "I'm in their way, it's that simple. I'm even more of a danger to them now that I'm tapped into the net."

"You make it sound terrible. At least you're here where we can keep an eye on you."

"Not for long, Madge. I've got to get out."

"No way, Roger. You're not nearly ready for that."

"I don't care if I'm ready or not. I've got work to do that I can only do in the field. Besides, if I don't get away from these walls soon I'll go stark raving mad."

Madge shook her head. "As your doctor, I can't let you leave."

"I'm not asking you, I'm telling you."

"Be sensible, Roger. We don't know what got to you out there. We can't risk exposing you again until you're stronger."

"I'm convinced it didn't have anything to do with the atmosphere. It *had* to be the trees. I'll just stay away from them."

"That's just your guess. It could have been the trees, but it could just as easily been almost anything else. This is a strange planet."

"It's the best guess I've got, and I'll go with it. Can you fix me up or not?"

Madge sighed, her shoulders slumped. "You need elements of both atmospheres as long as you're stuck in the middle. You'd have to wear an air supply."

"I'll do it," he said. "I have to get out of here."

"You'll need to have someone with you, someone you can rely on."

He looked up at her with a wry smile. "Do you have anyone to suggest?" he asked. "Aside from you and Sam, who around here can I really trust?"

"Teri," said Madge without hesitation. "You can trust Teri."

He nodded. That much was true.

It felt great to be outside again, to be able to feel the cool breezes against his skin. Everything looked new and fresh to Roger, alive. He'd been cooped up so long that even the trees looked good.

He and Teri walked slowly around the cultivated fields. His muscles were still sore, and he had a slight limp. They talked quietly. It has been a long time.

She was right, the fields looked good. But Roger had a feeling that it was only temporary. The area the trees gave up begrudgingly could be reclaimed overnight. Still, there was hope.

Roger stopped, pointed to the edge of the field. "Look," he said, as a fluffer disappeared into the trees.

"Ugh," said Teri. "Don't remind me. I told you what I saw out there. It was horrible."

"No," said Roger. "It was natural."

"I can't believe that. I *saw* it with my own eyes. The trees were killing the fluffers."

"No, they weren't. It's not that way at all.

What you saw wasn't the act of death, but just the opposite. They were giving life to each other. It's the way they exist, the way they've managed to survive all the changes on your planet."

"It was repulsive," said Teri, with a sour look on her face."

"I thought so, too. At least I did at first. Now I'm not too sure. In a way, it's beautiful."

"Beautiful? Ugh."

"You, of all people, Teri, ought to be able to see that."

"Me?"

"Sure. You're the one who thought the volcanos were beautiful, but they turned out to have their ugly side."

"Show me *anything* beautiful about a messed-up fluffer," said Teri. "I dare you."

Roger sat down on a log. He was still easily tired.

"Give me a minute," he said and Teri sat next to him. She nudged him with her elbow, caught up in a playful mood.

"Come on, tell me."

Roger leaned back and stroked the stubble on his chin beneath the loose-fitting oxygen mask he wore. His scars had mostly healed and he had started to grow a beard. Teri had been delighted when she discovered he could have hair on his face. He'd always seemed much too smooth. Roger was growing it for her. Personally, he hated the scratchy things.

"On Earth there's a plant that grows pretty

much everywhere. It has different names depending on where it's grown and what it looks like."

"Wait a minute. How can it look like anything but what it is? A plant's a plant, that's all."

"But this plant's pretty strange. It's grown for food, and when they grow it for the leaf it's called kale or cabbage. Kohlrabi is the stem. The flower produces cauliflower and broccoli. They all look different. If you saw them spread out on a table, you'd swear they couldn't be related, but they are. Essentially they're the same plant, right down to the genus and species."

"So what does this cabbage thing have to do with the fluffers?"

"I think the trees and fluffers are related in the same way that kale and cabbage are. They're different parts of a larger organism."

Teri looked at him with disbelief. "Are you trying to tell me that fluffers are plants?"

"Almost," said Roger. "At least I think they're part plant."

"I've never heard of such a thing."

"It happens sometimes, but seldom in such complex creatures. There's a microscopic organism called a Volvox which, by all definitions, should be a plant. It's a green sphere, just loaded with chlorophyll. Yet when you look closely, you find it's nothing but a colony of tiny one-celled animals acting like plants.

"Each of these little animals is more or less independent, but they subordinate their activities to benefit the colony as a whole. The Volvox can even move around, but only if everyone cooperates. The boundaries between plants and animals blur at this level. I'm no longer sure these boundaries even exist except as clever categories we've invented to lump things into."

"And what about the fluffers?"

"Their bone structure is actually closer to plant fibers than it is to normal calcium-based bones. Also, their metabolic system is such that they can't digest food without obtaining certain chlorophyll compounds from the trees. They get that at night, as you saw."

"Don't remind me." Teri shuddered and moved a little closer to Roger.

"The trees are complex, too, in more ways than we thought at first. Not only are they essential to the fluffers' life cycle, but they depend on the fluffers for their own existence. The trees need certain components that they derive from the fluffers' blood. They need each other. Neither the fluffers nor the trees could exist alone."

"There's a word for that, isn't there? Sim . . . sim . . . something like that."

"Symbiosis is what you're looking for, but that doesn't describe their real relationship. They don't simply depend on each other, they are *part* of each other, as related as kale and cabbage. Like the cells of the Volvox, they have different jobs to do, but the main thing is to keep the biomass alive. They seem to be doing a damn fine job of that."

Roger looked around him. He knew it was his imagination, but the trees seemed to be closing in on him. The nightmares touched his heart like ice. He couldn't shake a feeling of unfounded dread. It was a powerful system.

"It looks like they exchange more than nutrients at night. I think they actually pass genetic information back and forth between each other. That would explain how they can adapt to changing conditions so quickly. It's almost as if they completely reevaluate themselves every night. The fluffers move around a lot, so this genetic information is spread around the planet. The interlocking root system of the trees must play a part, too. It wouldn't surprise me to find out that the sea life is all part of the same chain. It's no wonder there have been so many problems with Frost. The planet presents a united front. You can't attack one part of it without attacking it as a whole."

"You make it sound hopeless." Teri's voice fell. Roger was sorry he'd talked so much. He hadn't meant to upset her. He was just trying to get things straight in his own mind. He rested his arm on her shoulder.

"It's not hopeless, Teri. In a way it may actually work to our advantage. There are things we can do—"

"Look," Teri interrupted. "We've got visitors."

Out of the sky a floater was bearing down on them. It was flying too low, coming in too fast. Roger grabbed Teri's arm.

"Run," he shouted.

Teri stumbled to her feet, confused. "What?" she said.

The floater leveled off about three meters above the ground and started spewing an ugly cloud of oily, yellow smoke. Roger recognized it as a highly caustic defoliant, outlawed on all the inhabited planets. The floater swung toward them and Roger pushed Teri along in front of him. The dome was an impossible distance away; the floater was closing in on them too fast. They cut to their right, heading for the trees. The floater followed them. They almost made it.

In the middle of a tight turn, the trailing fin of the floater clipped the branch of the tree. It just barely tapped it, but the contact was enough.

The unbalanced floater tipped steeply on its side, rapidly losing altitude as the pilot fought with the controls. The nose of the craft hit the ground, plowing a furrow twenty meters long before it disintegrated with a crushing explosion that sent shrapnel flying everywhere. Teri and Roger were lifted into the air by the force of the blast and tossed to the ground like rag dolls.

Roger shook his head and tried to clear it. His eyes burned and everything hurt like hell. He pushed himself to his knees and looked around for Teri.

She lay face down on the ground a short distance away, a terrible gash ripped from her hip to her shoulder where a piece of the

demolished floater had torn across her body.
She lay motionless in a rapidly spreading pool
of blood. Roger scrambled to her side and
stood there helplessly. In the distance alarm
bells rang from the direction of the dome. He
clenched his fists. *Damn it. Why her?*

Behind them, the body of Henry Sokol was
engulfed by the intense heat of the boiling fire
that destroyed the floater he had been piloting.

CHAPTER FOURTEEN

Madge swung the magnifier around and blinked the sweat out of her eyes. She worked smoothly and quickly, an island of calm in the middle of a storm of frantic activity. With intense concentration she carefully removed a small sliver of bone from Teri's fractured spine.

"Did you see how I worked that one out?" she asked.

The doctor standing to her side nodded, looking over her shoulder.

"There are six more in there," she said. "Do you think you can get them?"

"You slide them out?" he asked.

"That's right. Don't force them, ease them out. Some of them have jagged edges. Be careful of that nerve branch. It's almost hidden beneath the tissue."

"I see it," he said, moving around to take her place. "I'll get the rest of them."

A nurse on the other side of the makeshift operating table looked up, panic sweeping across her face. "Dr. Grinnell," she said, her voice cracking. "I can't stop the bleeding over here."

"Stay calm. I'll take a look."

Madge walked around to the nurse, threading her way through the maze of wires and tubing that trailed around the room like coiled snakes. This was one hell of a place to do surgery. It would have been better to lift Teri up to the station where they had proper equipment, but there had been no time. She wouldn't have survived the trip.

The table was surrounded by doctors and nurses. Several other medical personnel were crowded in the room, running machinery, monitoring the patient, or waiting to help. Teri was in the center, a clear canopy covering her, protecting her from infection as well as the harmful effects of normal air. The doctors and nurses worked through armholes in the canopy. There were never enough armholes and they always seemed to be in the wrong place.

Madge suctioned away the blood. Teri's tissue looked pink for a second, then red as more blood seeped in. The wound, to the right of her backbone and just above her hip, was deep, but not nearly as bad as some of the others.

"I'm going to fuse and pack this for now,"

said Madge, reaching for the cauterizer. "We'll have to come back later and fix it up, but this ought to hold it for now." Her hands moved quickly, expertly, with no wasted motion.

"How much blood has she had so far?"

"Eight units, Dr. Grinnell. Ninth going in right now."

Madge shook her head. They were really pumping it in, but she was losing it even faster. It looked grim.

"Step up the rate."

"We've already got it on full drip, Doctor."

"Then cuff it, damn it. She's still leaking. How's that belly tap?"

A doctor to one side looked up. "Not good," he said. "A lot of fluid coming out. Must be a mess in there."

"That's what I'm afraid of," said Madge. "But we'll have to go in now. Ease her over onto her back. Watch those lines, don't twist them."

This was the hard part. None of the other doctors knew much more about the pecularities of chimera anatomy than she did. It would be touch and go all the way, a lot of it just plain guesswork.

The possibilities for complications were enormous and frightening. Her neurological signs didn't look good. There could be major damage, internal injuries.

Madge caught her breath while the others finished prepping Teri. It seemed like they'd been working on the girl a long time already and the worst was just starting. Teri was strong to have held out this long. How much longer could she hold on, how much stronger was she?

Madge gritted her teeth and traced the first incision.

Roger had been pacing back and forth in the anteroom for over five hours. People in medical garb hurried in and out of the operating room, all business, never giving him any information. Finally, Madge walked out and slumped into a chair. Wearily, she pulled off her mask and shook her hair loose.

He looked at her, trying to read her face for some clue as to how it had gone. All he could see was fatigue. Her scrubs were splattered with blood. She looked thin and vulnerable, dead tired.

"I could use a cup of coffee, Roger." Madge's eyes were dull, staring straight ahead, half focused on nothing at all.

Roger went down the hall and located a coffee urn. Wherever there were doctors and nurses, there was always an endless supply of coffee and tea nearby. They went together. His hands shook as he poured two steaming cups. Cream and sugar for Madge, black for him. Patterns and routines established long ago, built brick by brick over the years. She'd sent him away so they could both gather their thoughts. He knew it, but it didn't matter.

She had washed up by the time he returned. Her hand was steady as she took her cup, but no amount of soap and water could erase the tiredness that etched her face. As she sipped her coffee, Roger scraped a chair across the floor and sat next to her.

"How bad was it?"

She closed her eyes tightly, shook her head.

"Is she alive?"

Madge sat her cup on the small table next to her. She nodded slowly.

"I'm not going to mince words with you, Roger. We've known each other too long for that. It was rough."

Roger felt a dull pain grab him in the gut. Madge had been through some bad ones and she wasn't prone to exaggeration.

"But she came through, right?" Grasping at straws.

"You could say that. Barely."

"What are her chances?"

Madge's eyes flared. "Look, goddamn it, I'm a surgeon, not a gambler. I don't play odds, I just do my job."

Roger snapped back in his chair. "I'm sorry," he said. "I didn't mean anything."

With a sigh Madge lowered her head and massaged her temples. She spoke though her hands and her tone was dull and level, drained of all emotion.

"No, I'm the one who's sorry, Roger. I shouldn't have jumped on you. I'm just tired and frustrated." She looked up again.

"She's got serious injuries and we've done all we can. I honestly don't know if it's enough. We were working in the dark and there was so much damage . . ." Her voice trailed off.

"The only reason she got through the operation is because she's strong. The only thing keeping her alive now is machines. Most of her systems have shut down. She's in deep shock. We've got her on a respirator and a dialysis unit is helping the only kidney she's got left. She's on the artificial heart, too. I tell you Roger, we pulled out all the stops. *I want her to live, too!*"

Madge slumped back in her chair and spread her hands in a formless gesture. "What more can I say? The machines can't keep her alive forever. She's right on the edge. It's all up to her."

Roger stared at his untouched coffee, his thoughts a jumbled mess. He felt helpless.

"So what are you going to do next, Roger?" asked Madge.

"Me?"

"You. You can't mope around here. That won't help anything."

Roger stood and paced silently across the room, trying to sort things out. He thought of the planet Teri loved and the things that had happened since he came. In his mind the fluffers and the trees became one, the entire planet became one unified organism, writhing and churning like a ball of green snakes. Hostile. He stopped and put his hand against the wall. It was cool to the touch.

"I have things to do," he said, making a conscious effort to organize his thoughts. "I have to talk with Holmes about the fluffers. I have to go topside."

"Good. It'll get your mind off Teri. I'll let you know if there's any change. There's really nothing you can do here."

"No," he said, still staring at his fingers pressed against the wall, his voice filled with sadness. "I guess there isn't."

Roger slept fitfully. After checking with Madge in the morning, he took a floater out to the small research station to see Eric Holmes, the scientist working with the fluffers. It was a short hop, and he found it difficult to concentrate on what he was doing. No change with Teri. He tried to focus on the business at hand. What he did in the next few hours was vitally important to Frost.

His pilot was Albert Hoff, chief of security for Unity's operations on Frost. Walsh had assigned him to keep an eye on him and Hoff took his orders literally. He'd slept in a chair next to Roger's bed last night.

Roger found the scientist in an observation room, taking notes while watching two fluffers through a glass wall. The fluffers seemed calm and relaxed, rolling colored blocks across the floor of their small room. Roger felt very much at ease with the man who had spent his life trying to protect native life forms from mankind's ruthless slaughter. They talked, and Roger told him that he'd come across his work in the datanet.

"That doesn't surprise me," said Eric. "It wasn't really confidential, but I didn't realize they'd be keeping such a close watch on me. *All* my data, you say?"

"Down to the last raw test score, as nearly as I can figure out."

Eric laughed easily and leaned back in his chair. "I'll bet they couldn't make any more sense out of it than I could."

"Maybe, maybe not," said Roger. "But your tests surprised me. I'd never seen the fluffers do anything that even hinted at advanced intelligence."

"I know," sighed Eric. "It's the same old story. They stand up and perform for my group, but they won't do it for anybody else. I suppose you think I fudged the data, too."

"No," said Roger, "nothing like that." He knew all about Eric's previous work and had nothing but respect for the man. "But I do think you influenced it."

"That's the same thing."

"No. I didn't say you did it purposely. I think it was inadvertent."

"That's simply not possible. If you saw the data you must have seen the controls we built into the experiments. I can't visualize any way the fluffers could have picked up cues from the person running the test."

"At first I couldn't either," said Roger. "The tests seemed well-controlled. There had to be some answer for the differences and I think I may have one. It started with something Teri told me."

"Teri?"

Roger paused. He felt a cold fear touch his heart.

"A friend," he said, trying to push the hurt away. "A chimera. She said the fluffers were skittish animals. I'd never noticed behavior like that at all."

"Neither have I."

"To me they were always neutral. They never showed the slightest fear or curiosity about me. Except once."

"What happened?"

"It was immediately after my accident. I was trying to get away and I felt isolated, terribly alone. I wanted companionship desperately. There were fluffers all around me, and for some reason they started acting friendly toward me. I no longer felt alone. It was almost as if they had sensed what I wanted, what I needed."

"Maybe," said Eric. "Or it could be that they were reacting to the stress situation in the same way that you were, desiring companionship. Perhaps you were interpreting their actions in the light of your own desires. It happens. I've seen it many times in my line of work."

"I know what you're saying, but I don't think that's the explanation. Teri wants to see skittish animals and she does. You want to see intelligent creatures and you do. Unity wants dumb animals and that's what they find. It doesn't matter to me and I get neutrality. Think about it."

"But how? And why?"

"I think the fluffers are empathic animals. They react to your feelings, your desires. They become what you want them to be. And the reason they do that is survival."

"Survival? I don't see it."

"They're very agreeable creatures. They behave just the way you would want them to behave. I'd say that's a pretty good survival characteristic in a variety of situations."

"That seems pretty farfetched," said Eric, frowning.

"Watch," said Roger, pointing to the two animals behind the one-way glass.

As he looked at them, Roger let his mind wander. He thought of Teri; battered, helpless, hovering near death. He thought of the planet that returned her love with violence. He concentrated on anger, distilling all the bitterness within him into a single point that burned with violence.

Eric was standing, his face inches from the glass. On the other side the two fluffers tore wildly around their room, teeth bared, striking out at everything within reach. They tore at each other, threw themselves against the wall, knocked the colored blocks around the floor.

"Damn," whispered Eric under his breath. "Damn."

Roger relaxed, rubbed his eyes. He felt the anger drain from his body, surprised at how easily it had come. Eric turned from the glass and faced him.

"Did you do that?" he asked.

Roger nodded.

"I've never seen anything like that before. We'll have to run tests." He looked back over his shoulder. The fluffers were calm again. "But I'm convinced," he said.

"So am I."

"But you don't think they're intelligent, do you?"

"No," said Roger. "At least not in the sense that you're looking for."

"Then they'll die." Eric sounded sad. "Unity will kill them off."

"I don't think so," said Roger. "I'm on my way up to see them. When they hear what I have to say I think they'll be very interested in keeping them alive."

Sam left his room, feeling out of sorts. He was restless. He'd been in orbit with nothing to do for too long, but cabin fever was only part of the problem.

He'd just talked with Roger, and as he wandered aimlessly through the halls, he worried about his boss. Roger was being torn up by something. He was obviously concerned about Teri; it showed on his face. But there was something deeper, something unresolved. Sam didn't know what it was, but he was sure it was important. He'd asked Madge the last time he'd called her and she had evaded the question. That was proof enough for him. Roger was up to talk with the brass at Unity, but Sam didn't want to go see him. It would be better to look him up later, alone. Maybe they'd share a bottle. Maybe they'd talk.

He walked into the lounge and looked around. It was too crowded. He sat in a booth with his back to the wall, trying to sink out of sight. He didn't want idle conversation, but at the same time he dreaded being alone. Too many things were nagging at him. A game of cards with a couple of friends would be nice, but he couldn't see anyone around he'd like to be with.

He felt closed in and helpless. There ought to be something he could do; for Roger, for Teri. There was nothing. He closed his eyes and tried to rest, but all he did was worry. When he opened his eyes he kept reading parts of random conversations in the lounge. He tried not to, but couldn't help it. He didn't go out of his way to eavesdrop, but sometimes it was just second nature, an automatic reaction to find out what was happening around him.

Sam had almost decided to move on when he saw Lou, a pilot for Unity, walk into the lounge. He caught his friend's attention with a wave of his arm. They talked across the room with their hands.

"What's happening?" signed Lou with one smooth motion.

"Nothing," signed Sam. "Absolutely zero. This place is getting to me."

"Let's go someplace else, then," signed Lou.

"Do you know of anything interesting happening?"

"No," signed Lou. "But if there is, we'll find

it. And if we can't find it, we'll make it ourselves."

They left together.

Morris Twelve wondered why the priest had asked him to come to the pits. The machine shop was a huge area, incredibly noisy. The shriek of machinery never stopped as metal was torn, drilled, ripped, and shaped. The smell of oil was heavy in the air. Darkened alcoves surrounded the main workshop. It was here that he had first met Drew, drowning in sin and squalor. The memory was painful, and the sound hurt his ears. When he saw the familiar robed figure he relaxed, but only a little.

The priest watched Morris approach. He had chosen this place so that their conversation would not be overheard. Time was about to run out. That fool Sokol had made one hell of a mess with his end. Security was getting tight and they were watching Trent like a hawk. This place was perfect—too noisy for a conversation to carry more than a very short distance. Most of the people wore earplugs in the pits, anyway, including the boozers, dopers, and card players on the far side of the workshop.

"Greetings, pilgrim," said the priest.

Morris made the sign of man in return. "You wanted me?" he asked.

"The church needs you. There is a job that needs to be done."

"Anything at all," said Morris, leaning

forward, straining to hear the priest above the noise. "I'm always at the church's disposal."

"It concerns the murder of your convert, Drew Seven."

Morris rocked back in shock. His hate and sorrow were very near the surface.

"We know who did it, pilgrim."

Morris reached out and grabbed the priest's arm.

"His name! Tell me his name. My brother's death must be avenged."

"His name is Roger Trent and his soul is loaded with sin. Not only is he responsible for the murder, but he lives among the chimera, walks among them, eats with them, loves with them."

Morris's rage grew. The man was evil, a monster.

"My obligation is plain," he said. "He has broken the holy bond between my convert and myself. *An eye for an eye, a soul for a soul,* as it is written. He must die."

"Would you do this with your own hand, pilgrim?" asked the priest.

"Of course." His eyes grew hard, his jaw was set. "This is my duty." Morris looked straight at the priest and paraphrased the words from the Book of the Way. "I must strike the hand that strikes my brother. His loss is my loss."

The priest handed Morris a small package. "This is your fist," he said. "Use it well."

Morris turned the package over in his hands.

"Trent is talking in the main conference room at this very minute. Do you know where that is?"

Morris nodded.

"What you hold is a bomb. Carry it to the meeting and place it under a seat in the back of the room. There is a small wire on the side. Pull the wire and get out of the room. It will go off five minutes later. Understand?"

"What if they won't let me in?" asked Morris.

"They will. They have to. As a registered lobbyist you have a right to attend the meeting as an observer. You won't be able to talk, but then, you won't have to."

"This will speak for me," he said, hefting the package. "It will speak for all of us. I know what to do."

"Go, then, pilgrim," said the priest.

"It's as good as done," said Morris, bowing his head slightly as he left.

The priest grinned with satisfaction at the retreating figure. He knew all along he'd been right in picking Morris to come to Frost. He was the perfect type for this job. Fanatics always were the best—they never questioned anything. Even if he happened to be caught, he would never admit anything, so deep was his feeling of obligation to the church. Of course, that wasn't anything to worry about. He'd never get caught.

There was no delay on the bomb. It would go as soon as he pulled the wire.

Morris would die with the rest of them,

thinking only of the church and revenge. The ironic thing was that he wasn't doing it for the church at all. He was just a small part of a complicated web that led someplace else, probably to an organization that stood to profit greatly if Unity should fail here at Frost. The priest was sure that he, in turn, would also profit.

Sam watched in stunned silence. He had sat out the last few hands of cards, not believing what his eyes were hearing. For although the room reverberated with ceaseless noise, that made no difference at all to him.

He'd been watching a conversation take place across the room. Sam had only been able to see one side of the conversation and hadn't caught all the words, but what he read from the lips of the priest was enough. More than enough. He left the table and started to follow the man out of the room.

The other players tried to tell him that he'd left his money sitting on the table, but he'd already turned his back and couldn't see them.

CHAPTER FIFTEEN

Roger experienced a small flash of *déjà vu* and shook it off. He was addressing much the same group of people he'd talked to when he first came to Frost. So much had happened since then, so much had changed. It seemed like years ago, a lifetime ago.

His mind was only half with the people in the room, the task at hand. The rest of his thoughts were with Teri. He'd checked in with Madge just before the meeting. There was still no word, no change in her condition. Damn.

His unwanted bodyguard, Hoff, was standing at the door in the rear of the large room, screening people as they entered. As far as Roger was concerned, it was a waste of time. If someone really wanted to get him they could do it without any difficulty. Walsh seemed to think that Sokol's death was the end of it, but

Roger wasn't convinced. Everything he'd seen indicated there were several people involved. They wouldn't stop until they got him or quit trying.

The rising bank of chairs beyond the table would seat over three hundred people, but most of them were empty. There weren't more than thirty or forty people in the room. It always seemed to be this way, thought Roger. Decisions that changed the lives of so many people were always made by a select few.

Walsh was showing the panic he obviously felt. The project was going badly and he was getting more and more pressure from his bosses back on Paragon. He wanted pat answers and easy solutions. He wanted them fast.

"That's all very good, Roger," he said. "I'm sure the scientists around this table are all quite interested in your theories about the interrelationships between the fluffers and the trees, but I fail to see what good that can possibly do us. The blurring of distinctions between our traditional concepts of plants and animals makes for fine intellectual debate, but we have very real problems here and we need practical answers."

"That's what I'm trying to give you," said Roger. "If you would shut your mouth for a moment and listen, you might learn something."

Walsh sat down, stunned at the force of Roger's words. People never ordered him around. He wasn't used to it.

"The trouble with you is that you've been

looking at the planet as an enemy too long and can't see anything else. You're locked into thinking of it as an adversary, an opponent, and interpret everything in those terms. It doesn't have to be that way at all. If you quit trying to kill everything off and looked at the planet with an eye toward using what's there, you might get someplace."

Dr. Mulhauser spoke up. "But Mr. Trent, you just got through telling us that the fluffers and the vegetation combine to react against everything we do. So how can we do anything else but fight it?"

"You can *use* it, turn it around. This planet reacts as a single entity and you've got to quit making it fight you. Start making it work for you. Take everything one step at a time. For example, look at the methane that's been giving you so much trouble. Methane is a biological product and is both produced and controlled by the biomass of the planet. What that means is that the methane is regulated by the fluffers and the vegetation. Instead of trying to fight back against the methane that's out there, you have to lead the system into producing less of it in the first place. The same thing is true of the excess nitrogen. This planet can't be forced. You can't work against it, the planet's too strong. You'll have to work with it."

"But methane and nitrogen are just two of the components that have been giving us trouble," said Dr. Mulhauser. "There are many, many more."

"And they're almost all organics," snapped Roger. "Guide the fluffers and the trees and you'll guide the planet. Most of the things that are giving you problems are reactions to the things you've done to the planet. Now you have to go back and undo them."

"Where would you suggest we start?" asked Walsh.

"Start at the beginning. Look at everything, and I mean *everything*. Go back to the basics, look at the original data. I already told you you'll have to weed out the incorrect information from the datanet, but that's just a start. I believe this planet can be turned around in two years. It'll take work, lots of it, but if you use the fluffers and trees to help, it can be done."

"Suppose you're right," said Walsh. "Do you have any specific suggestions? What would you do first?"

Roger opened a folder in front of him and passed some papers around the table.

"Like I said, we start at the beginning." He began to outline the broad plan he hoped would save Frost for Teri's people, but even as he went through the motions, his mind was someplace else.

Sam bulldozed his way across the cluttered floor of the pits, dodging machinery and shoving people out of his way. Oblivious to the shouts and curses hurled at him, he tried to keep the priest in sight. It was slow going; there were too many people. As the robed figure left the pits and turned the corner, a man grabbed Sam by the shoulder and spun him around.

"What do you think you're doing?" he shouted above the noise in the large room. The man wore a security badge and earplugs. Sam kicked him in the shins.

As the man hopped backwards clutching his leg and howling in pain, Sam sprinted to the exit. He caught a glimpse of the priest turning at the end of the corridor and ran toward him.

The priest heard Sam's footsteps echoing down the corridor and turned to see what the commotion was. By the time he realized what was happening, Sam was on him, knocking him to the floor.

"Where did he go?" yelled Sam. "The other one!" His voice, seldom used because he couldn't hear or control it, was garbled and distorted by emotion. What came out was more like a roar from some wild animal than words.

"Help." The priest was yelling, trying frantically to push Sam away. "Let me go, damn it. Help!"

Suddenly hands were all over Sam, pulling him roughly to his feet. Security men must have followed him from the pits.

"This man's crazy," said the priest, backing away from Sam. "He tried to kill me. He attacked me for no reason at all."

Two men held Sam, one on each side. They were both big men, heavyset. Sam couldn't hear them or talk to them. He felt, for the first time in years, a raging frustration at his inability to communicate. There was no time.

"We'll take care of him," said one of the men. "He won't bother you any more."

Sam quit struggling and felt the man on his right relax his grip. It wasn't much, but it was enough. Sam jabbed his elbow back as hard as he could, feeling it sink into the soft gut of the guard.

The man fell back, his breath knocked out of him. Sam took advantage of the momentary confusion to break away from the other guard. He started running. He had to get to Roger before the other man did.

Roger was anxious to finish things up. The shuttle was waiting for him. As soon as he was through with the meeting he'd be heading back down. It was time to tie up the loose ends. People were still coming in and out of the room. Out of the corner of his eye he saw Hoff let in a man in religious garb. He clarified a couple of points for Dr. Mulhauser, emphasized the importance of getting the datanet straightened out.

"Are there any more questions?" he asked.

"I don't think so," said Walsh. "At least not now. You've done an excellent job, Roger."

"I believe that's all I have for you today," he said, gathering up his papers. "From here it's back to the basics. You'll have to look at every single thing again. It's important to give up the idea of conquering Frost, because you'll

never be able to do that, no matter how hard
you try. But you can coexist with it, hand in
hand. It will take a lot of cooperation. You'll
have to try leading gently rather than forcing
your will on the planet. Frost will allow life,
but only life in harmony with the planet
itself."

Roger heard a noise at the back of the room
and looked up. Hoff was struggling with
someone, keeping him from coming in. With a
sudden shock, he saw the man was Sam. Before he could call out, Hoff was on the floor
and Sam was leaping over the chairs. What
the hell was going on?

Sam was wrestling with someone else now,
one of the spectators. He took a package away
from the man and threw it toward the door.
Hoff made a lunge for it, but it flew above his
outstretched hands into the corridor.

The room shook with the force of the explosion. Metal shrapnel and sparks were everywhere. People ducked for cover as the room
filled with dense black smoke. Harsh alarms
started to clang, reverberating against the
metal walls, almost drowning out the screams
of panic. Coughing, Roger anxiously scanned
the back of the room for Sam. Finally he saw his
friend through the smoke.

"Are you all right?" he signed.

Sam stood up and grinned. His face was
bloody and his nose looked broken. "I am
now," he signed.

*   *   *

"He'll have to make up his mind soon," signed Madge. "One way or the other, it can't wait much longer."

Sam's hands flew. He wasn't believing this. "You mean you'd cut him up and put him back together so he could live on Frost?"

Sam had come down to the planet's surface with Roger. He'd had more than enough of the station for a while. He and Madge were talking in her room. Roger was, as usual, sitting with Teri in another part of the complex.

"If he wants me to," signed Madge. "It's his decision."

"I guess that's what's been bothering him. That, and Teri."

"I would think so," signed Madge. "It's a big burden for one person to carry."

Sam paced around the small room, muttering to himself with his fingers. He turned to Madge. "What will you do?" he asked.

"You mean if he decides to go ahead?"

Sam shook his fist up and down: yes.

"Then I'll do the operation. It's my job."

"No, no. What will *you* do?" signed Sam. "With yourself?"

"I've been asking myself that same question lately."

"You're a good surgeon, one of the best. You could go anywhere, do anything. You could make a lot of money."

"Money's not everything," signed Madge. "I don't even have time to spend what I have now." She sat on the edge of her desk and straightened her pens.

"What would you do?" she asked.

"I don't know," signed Sam. "Get a job, I guess."

"You're a pretty good pilot."

"All pilots are good. There's no such thing as a bad one."

They looked at each other across the room. Sam took a step toward her and paused with uncertainty.

"It's not fair," he signed, half to himself.

"We've been together a long time," signed Madge.

"This isn't a bad place," he signed. "I might stay. They could use another pilot."

"You hate it here."

"I could sign up with Unity. That way I'd be in and out of Frost a lot. We could still see each other."

"What do you mean 'we'?"

"I'd be here almost half the time," he signed.

"I've been thinking a lot about the chimeras," signed Madge. "There's so much to do, so much to learn. They could use all the help they can get."

"I have some friends here, other pilots. It wouldn't be too bad."

"I could look at it as a professional challenge," she signed. "So much about the chimeras is unknown. They have interesting neurological pathways."

"We *have* been together a long time," signed Sam.

"A pretty good team," she signed.

"It would be a shame to break it up."

"I guess it's settled," she signed.

"What's settled?"

Madge looked at her old friend, a softness in her face. "If he stays, I'm staying."

Sam walked over to where she was sitting. He signed very slowly, with small quiet movements, almost a whisper in the air. "I'm staying too," he signed.

He touched her shoulder and she reached up and laid a hand on the side of his face. They held still for several seconds, caught in the moment. When the moment broke they hugged each other, first gently and tenderly, then harder. There were tears in Madge's eyes.

"I love you, old friend," Sam signed behind her back.

She couldn't see it, but she knew it in her heart.

There was nothing Roger could do but sit and wait. Teri hovered in the gray area between life and death. Machines kept her alive until her body could decide one way or the other. It was a long, seemingly endless wait, and Roger was at her side through it all.

Hours passed into days, marked only by the comings and goings of various doctors and nurses. The soft hum of the life support machinery was a low background murmur to that interminable period. Roger sat, and passed the time by thinking, trying to sort things out.

He watched Teri constantly, driving the nurses crazy. Every time she'd move a finger or moan in her unconscious state he would think she was coming out of it. There had been so many false alarms, all bringing hope to Roger and dashing it just as quickly. Being there only made it worse. Madge and the others had tried to get him to leave, but he'd refused.

He often thought of Teri's people and how hard they struggled to try to live on Frost, just as Teri struggled now. They never gave up, and that was something he admired about them.

Then there was Teri. He loved her.

There were other considerations. If he stayed on Frost, Madge had given him two years unless the planet came into line. Two years. Two years of what? Hard work and happiness? Heartbreak? Those were pretty long odds. Sam wouldn't touch them with a stick.

Sam. Sam and Madge. Old friends, he loved them both. The picture became confused, muddled. Old friends and new ones, the known against the unknown. Why was life so full of painful decisions? Why couldn't anything be clear-cut?

Teri moaned. Roger got out of his chair and went to the side of her bed. There had been other moans, but this one was different. She opened her eyes and looked around the room, focusing on Roger. She mouthed his name soundlessly, tried to reach out for him.

Tears fell from his eyes to the bed. He touched the side of her face, and she responded with a faint smile. All doubt was driven from his mind the instant he touched her.

He would stay.

CHAPTER SIXTEEN

Frost was slowly changing. The forces that had been pounding it for years had subsided, replaced by gentle nudges. The planet almost seemed to relax.

All Frost sought was a point of balance. That point could come anywhere along a broad range of possible conditions. Within that range was the place that Teri's people could live, the place that Unity was aiming for. They were approaching that place.

The atmosphere had cleared to the point that Teri and her people could spend up to a week outside without having to go through the detoxification procedure. This gave them the freedom to taste the planet and prepare for the day when it would be theirs.

The system was balancing out. A sense of

harmony was clearly felt between Unity's modification procedures and the planet. They coexisted, aiming toward a common point.

A fluffer sat on a lower branch of a tree. In its own way, that fluffer was tied to all the fluffers on the planet just as all the trees were tied together. They, in many ways, *were* Frost. The animal stared out over its planet with alert eyes.

A chimera walked quietly through the woods, taking notes on a small pad. He felt at home there, and the fluffer sensed that feeling as a vague sensation of comfortableness. The chimera was checking out the land he hoped some day to live upon. It felt good to be there.

The fluffer watched him from its perch. It did not run or hide because there was nothing to fear.

They both belonged in that place.

Mother Lei visited Teri several times while she was recovering. She felt awkward during these times with her daughter, but it was something she needed to do. Asking the impossible, she wanted Teri to understand her when she didn't even understand herself. Feeling out of place, she stood at the end of her daughter's bed.

"Teri, I'm sorry," she said.

"For what?" Teri was propped up in bed, still unable to stand. It had been a long and difficult recovery period.

"I haven't always been good to you." The words came hard; dredging up the feelings was even harder.

"You don't have to apologize," said Teri.

"I feel like I have to."

"You were only being the person you had to be," said Teri. "I was doing the same thing. Sometimes we clashed. Neither one of us could help it very much."

"Does knowing that help?"

"I think it does. It all helps." She looked at her mother for a long moment. "You never told me stories," she said in a soft voice. "Did your mothers ever tell you stories?"

Mother Lei smiled. "There are lots of stories," she said. "I never thought you'd be interested."

"What were they about?" asked Teri.

"Oh, little things, I guess. The things we did, the way we lived. One of my mother's sisters put a magnet on a computer console when she was a child. It took a month to unscramble everything. Little things."

"They're important to you, aren't they?"

Lei nodded.

"I want to hear them," said Teri. "Lan is interested, too. These things are a part of our lives and we should pay attention to them. Lan wants to write them down, save them. We can't turn our backs on the past."

Lei reached into the bag she was carrying and removed a small package. She gave it to Teri.

"I thought maybe you would want this," she said.

Teri opened it. "These are birth beads," she said.

Lei pointed to one of the black ones. "This is you," she said.

Teri held the string of small beads in her hand. There was life there, and death, a sense of place, a history. She was touched by her mother's gesture.

"There will be other children," she said. "A lot of children, I hope. It's a big world we're moving into."

"Maybe you'll be too busy for the beads, but I wanted you to have them."

"I don't think we'll be too busy," said Teri.

Lei brushed away a tear. "I . . . I love you," she said, choking back a sob. It was the first time she had said that.

"I love you, too," said Teri.

Mother Lei leaned over the bed and embraced her daughter. It was clumsy, awkward. But it was warm and honest. It felt good.

It was the first time they had done that, too.

On Paragon, the man known to some people as Nick was feeding papers into a small fire he'd started in the fireplace in his office. He was burning all the records he had of the connections between his employers and the Church of the One True Way. He'd already punched the code that automatically wiped the computer's memory of that fiasco. It was over, finished.

That fool priest had botched the job in grand style. He'd pay for that, and dearly. If Unity didn't nail him to the wall, there were plenty of others waiting to get their hands on him.

A lot of money had gone down the drain, but that didn't matter much. It was all a game, and at the level the megacorporations played, money wasn't nearly as important as power. They'd lost this skirmish, but there'd be others.

The connection between the priest and Nick was tenuous. He wasn't too worried about anything being tracked back to him. The lines from him to the next level were even more twisted. Everybody had covered their tracks well. He doubted that there was anyone who knew the full picture. Perhaps the lines even ran full circle back to Unity. Who could tell?

With a grim expression on his face, he tossed another scribbled note into the fire.

Roger walked up the beach, the sand crunching under his feet. It was cold, but he was used to it. The tide was out now, dead low, and the exposed sand bars were littered with shells and gnarled pieces of driftwood. The shells were oddly shaped, mostly spirals. He had one in his hand and was rubbing it unconsciously as he walked. He loved the ocean. It was such a peaceful place.

The patterns of the sea grabbed him and held him fast, as they always had, even back on Earth. He loved the cycles of storms and calm, the tides, the ever-changing face of the water. It was a constant reassurance that life went on. Even after a raging storm had rearranged the contours of the beach, the land still lived, the tides still ebbed and flowed.

He was busy these days, guiding Unity from the vantage point of the planet's surface. It gave him a good feel for what was happening. He liked what he saw. The planet was coming along nicely. They'd made more progress in the last few months than they had in the previous three decades. The planet felt right.

Frost belonged to Teri and her brothers and sisters. At times he felt like an outsider, but that was rare. The chimeras involved him in all their activities. Sometimes he even forgot he was different. Usually he felt like an adopted uncle.

There were days, though, when everything fell into place. At those special times he felt as though his whole life was interwoven with the very fabric of Frost. It felt natural and it felt good. He paid attention when it happened, and savored those times.

He still saw Sam and Madge fairly often, though his friends had to wear those bothersome suits. Sam felt he had to exaggerate all his signs to be understood through the suit. It was funny; he looked like a parody of a frantic white puppet. He'd taken over one of the Frost-to-Paragon runs for Unity. He said he liked it; that they didn't ride him as hard as Roger had.

Madge was working with the bioengineers on Frost. It was work she did well and her assistance speeded things up tremendously. Roger suspected her motives in staying around the planet were not purely professional, but he never told her that to her face. She'd probably deck him if he did.

Frost held the key to a lot of things. If the mechanism of the rapid genetic changeover was determined, it would open up a whole wealth of planets for mankind. If the process could be duplicated, a lot of things would change. Not only could Roger live on Frost indefinitely, but Teri could live on Earth. Mankind could live nearly anywhere. It was a dream, but one that they were looking at very closely.

Teri came down the beach, hobbling awkwardly in the brace that enclosed and supported her body. She wasn't used to it yet; that would take a lot longer. She would probably have to wear it for the rest of her life, but that bothered neither her nor Roger. It was simply a fact of life, something they lived with.

She reached him and they stood quietly together watching the waves, listening to the surf.

"Two years," she said. "Do you really think this can be ours in two years?"

Roger looked across the water and smelled the salty tang of the fresh sea breeze.

"I'm betting on it," he said, taking her hand in his.

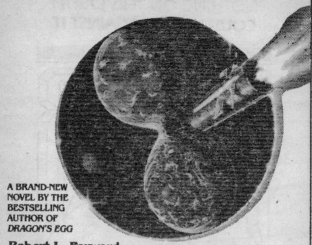

NOTHING ON THIS EARTH
COULD STAND AGAINST IT

DAVID DRAKE ☆ KARL EDWARD WAGNER

KILLER

Lycon was the greatest of the beast hunters
who fed the bloody maw of Rome's Coliseum.
How was he to know that the creature
he sought this time was not only as cunning
as he...but came from a world
more vicious than he could imagine?

288 pp. • $2.95

Distributed by Simon & Schuster
Mass Merchandise Sales Company
1230 Avenue of the Americas · New York, N.Y. 10020